MIRACULOUS JOURNEY

Further Stories and Songs of Milarepa,
Yogin, Poet, and Teacher of Tibet

Thirty-seven selections from the rare collection
*Stories and Songs from the Oral Tradition
of Jetsun Milarepa*

Translated by Lama Kunga Rimpoche
and
Brian Cutillo

LOTSAWA: 1986

Copyright © 1986 by Lama Kunga and Brian Cutillo
Illustrations on pages 2-3, 48-49, 116-117, 142-143, 176-177, 210
Copyright © 1986 Cynthia Moku

Library of Congress Cataloging in Publication Data

```
Mi-la-ras-pa, 1040-1123.
  Miraculous Journey.

  1. Spiritual life (Buddhism)  2. Buddhism--China--
Tibet.  I. Rimpoche, Kunga, Lama.  II. Cutillo, Brian.
III. Title.
BQ7950.M552  1986      294.3'83      86-27378
ISBN 0-932129-02-9
```

Editing: Kimberley Peterson
Cover art and illustrations: Cynthia Moku
Design: Merrill Peterson
Production: Matrix Productions
Typesetting: The Composing Room of Michigan, Inc.

ISBN: 0-932156-02-9

Printed in the United States of America

9 8 7 6 5 4 3 2 1

May this be an offering for those who seek alms,
A companion for those who wander the mountains,
Provision for those who travel the countryside,
And a sight for those who seek visions.

May it be a reception for those who arrive,
Company for those who stay,
And an escort for those who go.

In memory of Charles K. White

Contents

Lama Kunga

Foreword

by Lama Kunga Rimpoche,
formerly Thartse Shabdrung
of Ngor Monastery, Tibet

Many highly advanced people in earlier times
Endured hardships for the sake of Dharma in Tibet,
But I know of no one to equal you,
So rightly called "Mila, Lord of Yogins."

You, and the many practitioners of your lineage
Following after, traveled through time
To brighten the darkness, shining
Like stars in the sky of the Land of Snows.

But dark clouds of oppression from the east
Have hidden the beneficent sun from Tibetan people—
Just recently, since nineteen fifty-nine.
I still hope to see them vanish in my lifetime.

May those who contemplate, read, or just preserve
The well-kept message, the pure nectar of your teachings,
Which nourishes the lucky sons and daughters of your heart,
Realize the realm of reality, Mahamudra's goal,
And thus be inspired to give help to others.

Many young people in the West these days
Are of kind disposition and discerning mind;

Those interested in Dharma and history of Tibet
Should consider well the message of this book.

I myself have modest command of English.
Uncertain about my ability to translate
The topics in this book, both vast and deep,
I relied on the help of skillful translators
To transform these songs into English.
I offer them as a gift to the people of the West.

Acknowledgments

We would like to thank Dr. Nathan Sivin for providing the rare xylograph edition of the Tibetan text; Bea Ferrigno-Lee, Richard Kingerley, and Kim and Merrill Peterson for editorial advice; and George and Sarah Lukas, Alan Gevins, John E. Miller, William C. Mullich, and Daniel C. Kennedy for encouragement and support. We would also like to express our appreciation to Vivian Sinder who originally compiled the introductory material preceding each section.

All artwork is by Cynthia Moku, who has imbued the traditional Tibetan style of drawing with exceptional spontaneity and grace. She has been very understanding in collaborating with us to create a new Milarepa iconography.

Introduction

by Vivian Sinder and Brian Cutillo

The stories and songs of Milarepa are a rare record of an unusual man: yogin, poet, and spiritual teacher of eleventh-century Tibet. Although they reflect the cultural and religious traditions of his time, they are also a timeless testament to the practices and experiences of one person who achieved liberation through the Buddhist system of mental development. Using himself as living proof, Mila demonstrates the sources and signs of true spiritual achievement. He tells the story of his spiritual quest, vividly describing the hardships and adventures of transforming the human mind and condition into the clarity and bliss of the natural state. A summary of Milarepa's life, and of the basic principles of the Buddhist system of mental development, can be found in the introduction to *Drinking the Mountain Stream* (Lotsawa Press, 1978).

Milarepa's life (1052–1136) spanned the last half of the eleventh century and the beginning of the twelfth. His behavior, poetic imagery and style are colored by the customs and attitudes of his audience. Wandering the countryside, stopping at villages and encampments to sing in return for food, Mila was a bizarre figure to the people of Tibet. Yet he became a specifically Tibetan folk-hero who set an example of spiritual achievement that his Tibetan audience could understand. Even his more provocative and abrasive interactions reflect the Tibetan love for vigorous debate and spirited display, as well as their respect for the forceful aspects of power, whether possessed by deities, weather, charismatic people, or accomplished yogins. Nevertheless, his gift of example has a universal essence which makes his teaching relevant even into the twentieth century. Just as he sang for the people of his time, his songs still provide inspiration for spiritual development, and have become well known in the West.

Mila's perplexing behavior, often an arrogant caricature of common attitudes and customs, challenged his audience to expand their minds beyond the confines of conventional thinking. His responses to their questions frequently seem cryptic, for instead of answering directly, he dealt with the faulty thinking underlying the questions. Ultimately, however, there is only one true answer: the fact that the apparently independent existence of people and things is illusory; the natural state has been distorted by the conditioned perceptions of the ordinary mind. But because his listeners were at various stages of development, he used many different strategies. Mila's ability to affect his audience was due to his deep understanding of the workings of mind. His words and actions—even his occasional displays of supernormal powers—were practical approaches to specific problems. He manipulated the habit-bound workings of the conditioned mind with skillful thrusts aimed at the sources of mistaken concepts.

Mila's interactions established karmic connections with all sorts of people, enabling him to plant seeds for spiritual development in ways not always immediately comprehensible. The word *karma* means *action*. It refers to the operation of cause and effect *in the mind*; the complex network of past actions which conditions current perceptions and concepts, resulting in the habitual structuring of self and world. Any action, physical or mental, has repercussions within the realm of personal experience; each moment influences the next. Because the relationship between action and experience rules samsara, liberation is not attained by ignoring cause and effect. Instead, by working with it to create conditions conducive to spiritual growth, one creates a solid ground for the ultimate leap to freedom.

Expanding the mind into the unknown, especially through tantric techniques, is an ambitious and dangerous undertaking. Certain experiences on this path can divert the unprepared down wrong paths and even into madness. The guidance of a truly accomplished teacher is needed to bring practice and experience into focus, to help remove blockages and alter tactics according to the ever-changing condition of mind. Mila himself attributed the success of his practice to his teacher, Marpa the Translator (1012–1097), as attested by the dedication at the beginning of each song. On the other hand, it is said that without students to teach, there is no reason for a teacher to remain alive. Disciples of an ailing lama (teacher) beg him to stay by offering medicines and food and expressing their need for him. But material offerings are dispensable; the essential offering is the commitment of one's whole being to the task of liberation.

Compared with the typical image of a "spiritual teacher," Milarepa is a perplexing figure. He appears inconsistent and capricious in word and action because he lacks the "drone" of a stagnant personality. His freedom is not passivity, but spontaneous play in the natural state where everything— people and things, teacher and students—has lost the pretense of separate, independent, unchanging phenomena. The world of apparent phenomena is a mental distortion of reality due to the structuring of perception by the habits of the conditioned mind. By repeated meditative experience of the dissolution of these habitual fabrications, a yogin removes the *compulsion* to structure experience. In the natural state of mind he perceives the primordial and the ordered nature of things simultaneously. He is free to choose, and rather than reject the apparent world, he chooses to live within it, acting for the benefit of others with clear vision of both apparent and ultimate aspects. Such a person is called a *bodhisattva,* which means "enlightenment warrior." For a bodhisattva who understands the interconnectedness of all life, purely personal liberation is unthinkable. In the social world one's role cannot be changed unless the attitudes of others concerning that role are also changed. Likewise, a bodhisattva realizes that his spiritual development is inextricably bound to the development of others. He uses this bond to enact the drama of his life and maintain the ability to relate to others in order to show them the way to freedom. A realized person like Mila is not an impersonal shell, incapable of emotion and friendship; his truly human nature must always be remembered. Mila's concerns were constantly focused on the development of those around him. In the manner of a powerful dramatist or improvisational actor, his words and actions skillfully enlarged the scope of others' perceptions and concepts, gradually loosening the hard earth of their rigid, ingrained patterns of thinking.

The popularity of Milarepa's songs, which has continued to the present time, is the playing out of his bodhisattva commitment. He sang not just to provide entertainment in the vast and lonely expanses of Tibet, but as a public service, a craft for the benefit of others. Like the crafts practiced by the tantric siddhas of India, Mila's "aimless wanderings" were actually as deliberate as weaving cloth, building a bridge, or plowing a field. His attainment of enlightenment was an exceptional achievement, but his extraordinary awareness of the needs of others and his ability to guide them toward liberation make Mila's life truly miraculous. His compassionate concern reached beyond his lifetime with an energy central to the aspirations of all humankind. The Buddha predicted that in later ages the human condition would degenerate and social attitudes would become materialistic and confused, but that in such difficult times there would be teachers of extraordinary power, able to take radical approaches to the teaching of Dharma. In making Buddhist teachings alive for us, such teachers are said to be more helpful than the Buddha himself. Milarepa's time was such a time, as is ours.

Translator's Note

We do not know how accurately Milarepa's words are preserved in oral tradition and transcribed texts. Variant versions of the same story exist and similar passages occur in different songs. Stylistic differences are found both between pieces and within the same story. A few songs contain lengthy passages of inferior content and quality—probably added by storytellers during the three centuries before the oral versions were transcribed. Some pieces are polished expositions of theoretical topics; they lack the spontaneity of most of the songs—perhaps the result of editing and polishing during preparation of the written texts. However, most songs contain short passages of penetrating insight and vivid imagery. This is especially evident in the present work, where the unembellished, spontaneous style of such passages resembles the esoteric songs (dohas) of the tantric yogins of India. Perhaps these fragments are the best record of Mila's actual words, easily remembered kernels around which later material developed.

This book, together with *Drinking the Mountain Stream* (Lotsawa, 1978), comprises the first translation of the rare collection entitled *Stories and Songs from the Oral Tradition of Jetsun Milarepa* (Tib. rJe.btsun Mi.la.ras.pa'i rDo.rje'i.mgur.druk.sogs gSung.rgyun.thor.bu.pa.'ga'). The text provides only two pieces of evidence about the date and circumstances of its preparation. First, the colophon states:

> This rain of nectar of the clouds of dharma
> Fell from the monastery of Trashi Kyil
> So fortunate farmers wherever Buddha's teachings are sown
> May reap crops of happiness and joy.

This indicates that the wooden xylograph blocks were carved at Lha.ram. bkras.shis.gyas.su.'khyil, a large monastic center of learning in north-eastern Tibet.

Second, the group of songs at the beginning of the text, subtitled "Six Vajra Songs," has a preface stating that their publication was directed by lHai.bTsun.pa Rin.chen rNam.rgyal of Brag.dKar (1473–1557), who was also the author of the biography of Naropa translated into English by Dr. Herbert Guenther (*The Life and Teachings of Naropa*, Oxford University Press, 1973). It is not clear whether this attribution extends to the rest of the volume, or what role Rin.chen rNam.ryal had in its production. Rin.chen rNam.rgyal was a colleague of Tsang Nyon Heruka (1452–1507), who produced the *100,000 Songs* and the *Autobiography* of Milarepa. It is possible that he had access to the transcriptions made from oral informants during preparation of the *100,000 Songs* and, in particular, to material not included in that collection. The text translated here may have been compiled from such "pieces from the cutting-room floor." This conjecture is supported by the comment "printed afterwards" or "later" in the above-mentioned preface, and by the expression "some bits and pieces" (thor. bu.pa.agaa) on the title page. The present text differs from the *100,000 Songs*; it is more spontaneous and resembles raw, unedited transcriptions. Some pieces are fragmentary, and one such fragment states explicitly that it is material left out of a chapter of the *100,000 Songs*, as does the chapter "Confrontation with a Bon Priest" in *Drinking the Mountain Stream*. In "Song of the Peacock" the characters and plot differ from the version in the *100,000 Songs* (Chapter 8), and "Mila Guides His Mother's Spirit" is a condensation of two separate songs in the other collection (*100,000 Songs*, Chapter 54). However, almost all the material in the present volume is completely different from anything in the *Songs* or the *Autobiography*. It is of good quality and complements the information in the better known works.

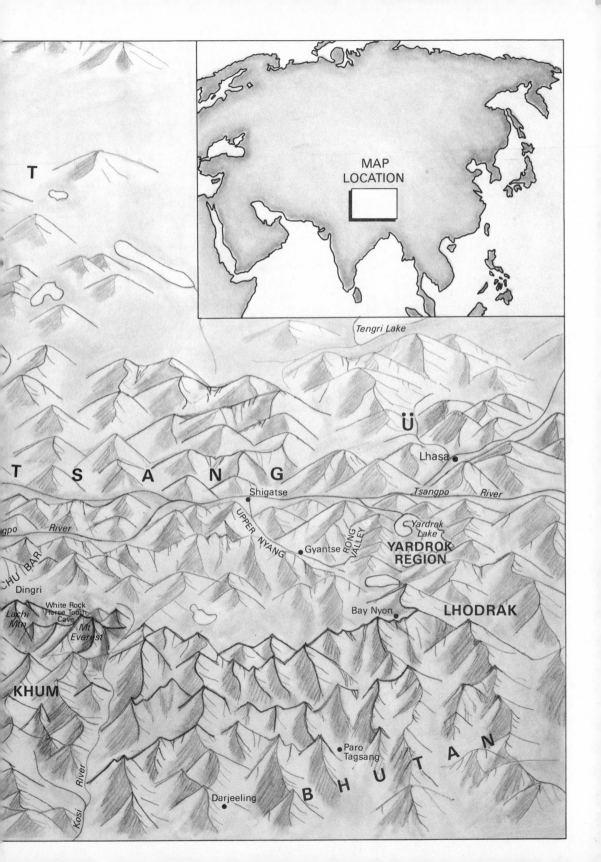

T

MAP
LOCATION

Tengri Lake

Ü

Lhasa

T   S   A   N   G

Shigatse   Tsangpo   River

UPPER
NYANG   Yardrok
Lake

gpo   River   Gyantse   RONG
VALLEY   YARDROK
CHU BAR   REGION

Dingri   Bay Nyon   LHODRAK

White Rock
Horse Tooth
Cave
Lachi
Mtn   Mt
Everest

KHUM

Kosi
River

Paro
Tagsang

Darjeeling   B   H   U   T   A   N

PART ONE

JOURNEY SONGS

The Journey

Travel was the medium for Jetsun Milarepa's extraordinary life-work: to achieve spiritual liberation and guide others on their journey to freedom. Although he praised the life of solitary meditation, Mila frequently exposed himself to the rigors of travel. Although he claimed this was to avoid bothersome visitors, his travels brought him into contact with many people in all walks of life, providing them the opportunity of meeting a truly liberated person. Had he remained in isolated retreats, he could not have fulfilled his vision of establishing a valid lineage of buddhist practice on Tibetan soil. Through the medium of journey his spiritual achievement became public knowledge, fostering an awareness of the possibility of freedom indelibly impressed on Tibetan culture. The paradox between private and public aspects of this homeless yogin reflects the conflict between self-development and social responsibility which every practitioner must face. Mila shows us that ultimately there is no conflict: for practice to be successful, social and solitary aspects *must* be integrated.

Mila responded to the specific needs of each person. His ability to balance meditation and action, present concerns and timeless truths, is especially impressive in view of the transitional nature of the time, when buddhist teachings were relatively new and poorly understood. In establishing rapport with an audience he was sometimes aggressive, as in "The Hostile Herdsmen," and sometimes cordial, as in "Invitation to the Feast." Occasionally he would mimic local customs or religion in exaggerated detail. Throughout, he wove his message subtly into the fabric of his performance. He used the curiosity and antagonism provoked by his scanty clothing, emaciated body, and eccentric behavior as a starting point for explaining deeper differences between himself and his audience. The success of Mila's actions, balanced precisely at the convergence of worldly life and inexpressible reality, are due in part to his skill in timing. As he says in "Song of Escort," "If you observe a bird's flight you will understand timing." You must understand your own mind, at least to some degree, before you can understand and improve the minds of others. And in turn, worldly experience when properly understood is a valuable aid to spiritual development. They are as closely related as the up and down strokes of a bird's wing.

Mila's travels exemplify a practitioner's journey through samsara to liberation and the bodhisattva's return to guide others to freedom. Though he knew that the source of liberation is within, he continued to move through the world of appearances. Playing the wandering, homeless stranger, he made the only trip he considered worthwhile—to the natural state of mind, where one is in harmony with all beings and things. His freedom was his independence from going or staying. His accomplishment was the balancing of life in the ordinary world with an intense inner vision; his ability to reach out and assist, in the face of devastating realization, the spiritual journey of others.

Invitation to the Feast

The 100,000 Songs *contains the well-known story of the contest of spiritual skills between Jetsun Milarepa and a shaman of the indigenous Tibetan religion, called* Bon, *which took place on Mt. Tisay (Mt. Kailash). Mila defeated the shaman and claimed the mountain as a site for buddhist practice. The first five stories are from the group of pieces subtitled "Six Vajra Songs" which tells of Mila's return from practicing at Mt. Tisay. (The remaining material is in* Drinking the Mountain Stream, *chapter 14).*

After staying on Mount Tisay, Jetsun Milarepa and his disciple Rechungpa resumed their journey. Along the way they met a large group of herdsmen and went to beg food. One of the herdsmen, a young man named Gyegong Bum, had just been married and the wedding was being celebrated with a feast of meat from many slaughtered animals, including wild and domestic yak, and sheep, along with much beer. Everyone was singing and playing and teacher and disciple went to join the feast. A patron approached them, offered beer, and said, "We're all celebrating. Until tomorrow morning it is the custom that offerings for the feast be exchanged, but since you're both ascetics and cannot reciprocate with food, perhaps you can offer a song of your experiences?" So Jetsun sang this song:

> I bow to my lama, the wish-granting gem,
> Abiding in the changeless dharma-realm,
> Who satisfies all desires and inner needs
> Of those who pray to you.

Now you patrons gathered here
Stop your chatter, hear this song,
And consider its meaning carefully.

You adults, youths, and children sang your songs;
I the yogin will sing one too.
You have all exchanged offerings of food;
I the yogin will exchange some too.
This is my way of reciprocating:

At the beginning of my spiritual journey,
I alternated between states of ordinary awareness
And unobstructed voidness
Until I became enlightened,
And realized that the voidness experienced through meditation
    practice
Is no different than the natural voidness of reality.

Mounted on the horse of supplication
Born from the stores of merit and gnosis
My perfect enjoyment-body
Trained a pure circle of students
In densely packed Akanishta Heaven,
While my emanation-body sprung from it
Is here! Invite me to the feast!

The big yak, born of ignorance,
Synthesis, consciousness, mind and matter, and so on,[1]
Fills two-thirds of all the world.
The draught flowing from the mind-for-enlightenment
Fills the remainder of this world to the brim.

I lead this great yak to slaughter.
I emanate beings possessed of strength
Who press to his head the iron goad,
Bind him well with vajra-shackles,
And tie him tight with stout iron chain.

8

I plunge to his heart the sword of wisdom,
Slaughter him with the knife of concentration,
And divide him up into symbols of spiritual progress.
Through my achievement of self-clarity,
I now call the guests to join the feast:

Here in this part of the human realm
Four types of guest are gathered:
In the air above the feasting ground,
Within the vast mansion of wisdom,
The Three Gems attend as honored guests.
Below them, and seated all around,
Worthy Dharma Protectors take their places.
On the earth of this material world
The six types of pitiful beings assemble,
And among them, wherever they find a spot,
Sit those burdened with the blood-hatred of karmic debts.

Now for my "reciprocation" I offer this feast:
Within this great yak's skull,
So large and broad
And well proportioned,
The brain becomes a sea of pure nectar
Awash with the blessed waves of five types of flesh,
Five types of nectar, and the fivefold wisdom.
Receive this offering with pleasure,
Host of enjoyment-bodied Conquerors!

On the strength of such offerings and devotion
To my honored guests, may all beings,
Led by those present here,
Complete their stores and cleanse obscurations.
May they acquire merit and enjoy the bliss of advancement,
And attain liberation in the end.

Then, to the worthy guests—
The hosts of protectors and preservers,

I offer a feast of sacred nectars,
The essences of this great yak's flesh:
Blood, fat, bone and marrow,
Along with the first portions of sacred fluids.
May they accept this agreeable feast,
Protect and preserve the doctrine,
And may those who uphold the teachings
Be steadfast and blessed with happiness.

Then, with their shares of this big yak's meat,
May all pitiful creatures of the six realms,
Without exception, be fulfilled
In their need for food and drink
Each according to his own desire.
May their needs be satisfied,
Their minds and bodies filled with bliss,
And, after relief from all pain,
May they attain liberation in the end.

Then, to the guests with karmic debts,
I dedicate the portions of meat
Which fulfill all desires,
Thus repaying the karmic debts acquired
Since beginningless time until now.
May these guests be filled with good intentions,
Through the quenching of vindictiveness,
And attain the high state of omniscience.

With what's left from thus repaying
All four types of guest
I'll reciprocate and entertain
All you patrons present here.

First to this boy, my host,
With his household and family,
I serve heart, liver, and other organs—
The inner flesh of six purified senses—

Heaped upon a fivefold portion
Of meat cleansed of five poisonous afflictions.

Then, to the upper row of guests
I serve the inner organs heaped
On twofold portions of both stores complete.

To those at the end of line
I serve the inner organs
On a dish of many tastes combined.

Finally, I serve this drink of mind-for-enlightenment,
In measured amounts,
According to the servings of meat;
And those elemental spirits unexpectedly come,
Famished and weak in strength,
I also satisfy with modest portions.
May all, body and mind filled with bliss,
Attain the high station of Buddhahood.

Thus the yogin Milarepa,
With this mass of slaughtered yak meat
Which was once the vehicle of sentient mind,
And with the drink of enlightenment-mind,
Prepared a circle feast of offerings
And offered it up symbolically.

Lama and Triple Gem, receive this devotion!
Protectors and preservers, don't desert us!
Grant us blessings, honored guests!
Remove obstructions, worthy guests!
Complete both stores, pitiful guests!
Accept this repayment of karmic debts!
Receive this exchange of food
All patrons gathered here.

Listen again, gods and people:
I know all appearance is illusion,
And illusion merely wrong perception.
With illusory action everything is possible.

Between your celebration of materiality,
Your mere superficial reality,
And my celebration of indentitylessness
In the state of absolute reality,
The difference is as great as the difference between
The palm of your hand and the sky.

You believe illusion to be reality;
I believe reality is illusion.
Slaughtering illusory "animals," I eat without fault
And drink the heady blend of evil poisons.
I prepare myself for the Hell of Repeated Revival[2]
And jump, eyes open, into the abyss of low states.

But if you also think to consume meat and beer
And take your chances in lower states,
Consider: my body, in a great palace,
Offers the worship of burnt offerings
To a host of peerless Mantra deities
And seals it with impartial dedication.
You eat out of a perverse desire and craving;
If you copy me you will court disaster.

I am yogin Milarepa—
You may think me unhappy, but I'm full of bliss.
In summer, I'm blissful in the mountains;
In winter, blissful in the forests;
In spring, I'm blissful in the canyons;
In autumn, blissful begging alms.

I'm happy whatever appearances show their faces.
Whatever happens, I rejoice in reality's freedom.

Because the world shines divinely, I'm happy.
In whatever I do, I'm happy.

Careful! Careful! Gods and people!
Unable to bear the pain of a thorn,
You feed off others' slaughtered lives.
Beware the pains of the Hell of Repeated Revival—
Gooseflesh at the scorching of your skin.

Unable to bear hot melted butter,
You drink intoxicating, evil beer.
Have a thought for the boiling copper—
Gooseflesh at the scalding of your guts.

Your sin-food—fatty meat—
Is still there; I've not touched it.
Take it yourselves if it pleases you.
Hold out your cups to collect what I owe—
Your intoxicating, poisonous venom: beer.

Singing this, Milarepa rose eighteen feet into the air. He shook his hands, and honey nectar rained from his fingertips, filling all empty vessels to the brim. Everyone was awestruck. They bowed and circled him, saying, "Jetsun Milarepa, we did not know you."

After preparing a high cushion, they begged him, "Now in your mercy for us, please be seated on this throne." He went and sat on the throne and distributed the beer equally from the vessels. Its flavor was excellent, filling mind and body with bliss; it swept away the previous alcohol intoxication, clarifying senses and mind.

Again, everyone bowed to him, exclaiming, "A buddha has come to our door—we must have some fortune. Please teach us Dharma." So Jetsun taught them about the cause-and-effect relationship of actions and initiated them into the six-syllable mantra OM MANI PADME HUM.

After three days he prepared to leave. The elder patrons entreated, "Jetsun lama, please stay for a year, or for a month, or at least a few days." So Mila remained a few more days. The people promised not to hunt and to refrain totally from taking life, and also took the vows of refuge and Mani-mantra.

When he was about to leave he sang this song:

To translator Marpa's feet I bow,
Emanation-body of great Vajradhara,
Bless the followers who rely on me
To keep their minds on Dharma.

Listen attentively, faithful ones:
The outcome of birth is death;
Life will not endure.
If you die this very day,
What comfort will you find in mind?
Have no regrets in the face of death.

The outcome of accumulation is dispersion;
Limbs and joints will fall apart.
Why even speak of ephemeral friends?
Abandon partiality toward everyone.
Make compassion and wisdom inseparable friends.

At the end of acquisition comes loss;
Material wealth slips away,
And what little remains must be left behind.
Now, while you have the chance,
Give gifts ceaselessly,
For this causes rebirth in happy states.

Three auspicious dates—the first, eighth, and fifteenth—
Are the religious share of laymen;
On them keep the vows of abstinence,[3]
Refrain, however you are able, from what is evil,
Prohibited, or naturally sinful,
And practice virtue in body, speech and mind.

Through the karmic connection of previous lives
We have come together in the present;

Through our contact in this life,
May we next meet in a pure realm
To practice Dharma.

May you abandon evil and cultivate virtue,
And have the fortune of winning freedom.

Bandits of Mind

After traveling about three days more, Milarepa and Rechungpa came to a trail that led through a narrow ravine, a typical place for bandits to wait. Rechungpa cried, "We had better hurry. Bandits may be waiting in this ravine."

In reply, Milarepa sang this song:

To translator Marpa,
My precious lama and sole protection
From all fears, I pray:
Empower me to melt the ice of my mind.

Through beginningless time we've lived
In the narrow ravine of lower states
On the vast plain of samsara.

Sometimes the bandit of intense hatred overtook us,
Dragged us to the depths of hell,
And tortured us by boiling, burning, cutting—
Or cast us into a dark wasteland of ice.
Where the intensely cold winds froze us.

Sometimes the bandit of intense desire overtook us,
Dragged us to the low state of frustrated spirits,
And tormented us with unbelievable hunger and thirst.

Sometimes the bandit of delusion overtook us,
Dragged us to the low state of animals,
Mired us in unbearable stupidity and slaughtered us.

Through beginningless time
We've endured the pain of low states,
Seldom born in the three higher states
For a moment's rest or to do meaningful work.

Why should we now be afraid to stay
In this ravine in the realm of men?
In fact, when you've got nothing
You are free of all enemies;
Let those bandits do as they please!

Bagtsa Gonay

Once when Mila and Rechungpa were focused in the natural state, a large party of traders arrived at their campsite laden with fresh meat. One of them said, "Here are two emaciated ascetics! They don't even seem to have provisions in this desolate place. What pale complexions! What clothes! Pitiful! Let's give them some food."

They offered a good quantity of meat. Mila said, "I acknowledge your gift, but I do not eat slaughtered meat. Take it back."

A trader replied, "You don't eat slaughtered meat! Well, unslaughtered meat won't arrive of its own accord. And isn't your rejection itself enough to kill? There is no need to feel sorry for such creatures!"

So Jetsun sang them this song:

> Precious lama, my guide in this life and next,
> I pray, grant me blessings.
>
> This illusory stallion of mind and currents
> I saddle and harness with awareness and judgment,
> And I myself, the yogin, ride on him.
>
> I sling on packs of provisions for giving,
> Wear the fine uniform of morality,
> And bear the armor of patience upon my back.
>
> I drive this steed with the whip of vigor,
> Eat the food of superb absorption,
> And shoulder the bow and arrow of method and wisdom.

Over the vast plain of great bliss
I track the great yak of the three virulent poisons.
With the method-feathered arrow of wisdom
I pierce the heart of this egotistical yak.
And divide its meat of egolessness
Among beloved friends in the six worldy conditions.

After hearing this song, a man named Bagtsa Gonay dismounted and
approached Mila. "Tell me yogin, where have you come from? Where are
you going? What is your name?"

In reply, Mila sang another song:

Homage to my father-lamas;
Pray protect us sinners.

Now listen closely, patrons,
As I answer Bagtsa's questions.

My birthplace was lower Gung Thang plateau,
I went to study in Ü and Tsang.
My burden of bad karma was ended in Ngok of Mar.

I received all four mantric empowerments,
Worked with my currents, channels, and drops;
And developed the receptive state of mahamudra.

I left the province of Tsang
And went to snowy Tisay mountain,
Where I survived by chewing the stones of austerity,
While I cultivated the experience of the natural state
Until realization of reality was born within.

My name is Yogin Milarepa,
My disciple's name is Rechungpa Repa.
We're headed now to the region of Lachi.

Your consciousness propelled by ignorant action,
In illusory bodies composed of four illusory elements,
Wanders the illusory city of the six samsaric states.

Habituated to base instincts from beginningless time,
You are obsessed with food, drink, and wealth.

Driven to the ten evil actions,
Like slaughtering others through desire,
You will stray in the future to even lower states
And experience their unbearable pains.

Thus I, the aimless yogin,
Feel pity for you.
You in turn feel pity for me—
We're just swapping feelings of pity!

I pray you have the fortune to find dharma.
I now depart for wherever I'm going.

Stuck with strong faith, they gathered all the barley meal they had and said, "Wise lama, as you do not eat meat, why not accept this barley meal? Our village is just a day's journey away; please come."

"I will not go to your village, and I do not have a container for this barley meal so please take it back. I'll eat just a pinch to establish a food connection with you."

"We will give you a container; we insist that you accept our offering. Now that we have seen you with our own eyes and heard you with our own ears, please teach us a little dharma."

So Mila taught them about the cause-and-effect relationship of action. They made the commitment not to kill and took vows to practice the mantra OM MANI PADME HUM. Then Mila sang this song:

The sight of your body clears obstructions of body,
The sound of your voice clears obstructions of speech,
Your mind is the essence of impartial love;
Protect me with your body, speech and mind.

Life dwindles with each passing moment,
Diminishing constantly by day, month and year.
There is no certainty about the time of death
So repeat the Mani-mantra, courageous friends.

Through the force of habituation to base instincts
Unintentional evil and sin can occur.
Keep careful watch with awareness and judgment,
And cease evil actions, courageous friends.

After death, all wealth, all friends—
Anything save dharma—are of no use.
Thus now, while you've the chance,
Gather merit, courageous friends.

After singing this, Mila left. Later on, while he was staying in Nyanam, Bagtsa Gonay joined him, and after receiving the essential dharma, empowerments and instructions for practice, he became an excellent yogin.

Mila and the Fierce Dogs

Mila and Rechungpa continued their journey together. Late one morning they entered a scattered settlement of herdsmen and approached the area used as a village square. "Hey! Give some hot food to two hungry yogins," Mila cried.

One man replied, "Usually puny beggars cannot get past our guard dogs, but now they're not even attacking! You must have an effective spell for subduing dogs. Do not try to rob us tonight."

So Jetsun sang this song:

> I pray to my supreme lama
> Whose compassion touches all beings.
>
> By developing both aspects of enlightenment-mind[4]
> My love is such that dogs don't attack me.
> Have no fear of being robbed by me—
> A pauper who's quit clinging to ego and wealth.
> There *is* a bandit here right now—but it's not me!
> Keep a careful watch out for him!
>
> At the borderline of in- and out-breath
> The rope of life is just a thread.
> Here, the bandit of obstructions dogs you,
> Leading closer moment by moment,
> The agents of the Lord of Death.
> Through passing days, months and years

He'll surely rob the force of life.
Isn't it best to hide it securely
In the deathless, primal clear-light of mind?

At the borderline of samsara and nirvana
The precious, fulfilling gem of merit
Lies in the vulnerable house of mind.
Led on by the ten kinds of evil action,
Agents sent by past bad behavior,
Bandits which are the five poisonous afflictions
Will surely rob your gem of merit.
Isn't it best to stash it well
In the wisdom-treasury of the two stores complete?

At the line between ordinary and transcendent awareness
Lies the tiny seed of true being.
Led by the torrent of negative thoughts,
The agents of ignorance—
Demonic bandits of belief in identities—
Will surely rob the seed of true being,
While you're stuck in concepts of ego.
Isn't it best to hide it well
In gnostic awareness of the natural state?

Thus a tight tongue in a closed mouth
Is my [silent] precept to you.
If understood, it's a priceless gem;
If not, it's a thorn piercing the ear.

These lines were composed in my humble mind,
But they express the thought of the Conquerors of time.
Drink deep of their melody, worthy patrons.

I pray you have the fortune to follow Dharma
And be virtuous. And remember:
All composed things are like a star,
A defect of eye, mirage and dew,
Like bubbles, dreams, lightning, mist, and clouds.

An elder exclaimed, "Amazing! Where are you from?" He asked many more questions and after Mila had answered them all the elder cried, "Jetsun Milarepa and his disciple! I did not know you." He paid respects, circled them, and offered yoghurt with butter cakes.

Mila told him, "I appreciate your gift of yogin's food, but I don't even have a container to hold these butter cakes. You keep them."

But the elder replied, "If you can not take these offerings with you, please stay three days so we may serve you." At this fervent request, Mila agreed to stay for three days. He taught Dharma and gave initiations into the practice of the six-syllable Mani-mantra. As he was about to leave, he offered this benediction:

> Lamas, personal deities,
> Buddhas and Bodhisattvas of the ten directions:
> Remember me and my patrons.
>
> Patrons and fine company,
> On the strength of the services you've provided
> To these two beggar yogins,
> May the teachings flourish here
> And the intentions of the Buddhas be achieved.
> May you always live in the presence
> Of the bearers of the doctrine.
>
> May the community of dharma practitioners grow strong,
> May this land be endowed with happiness and bliss,
> May obstructive conditions be removed,
> And conditions be right for spiritual practice.
>
> May you patrons, especially, totally cleanse
> Your obstruction of accumulated bad actions.
> May you complete the stores of merit and gnosis,
> And obtain the body of Omniscient Conqueror.
>
> May you enjoy bliss through meritorious action,
> Untouched by inadvertent evil,
> And in the end attain the high state
> Of a Conqueror possessing ultimate gnosis.

May you enjoy the physical fortune of voidness of forms,
The verbal fortune of the voidness of sounds,
The mental fortune of lucent voidness,
And the fortune to recite the Mani-mantra.

And after perfecting the completion phase
Unswayed from the three types of behavioral practice[5]
While in the production phase of five realizations,[6]
May you have fortune like that of Avalokiteshvara.

The Hostile Herdsmen

Continuing their travels, Mila and Rechungpa came to a pleasant broad valley where a river flowed through lush grasses. Mila said, "Oh Rechungpa, let's stay here for a day," and they did. As they enjoyed the warm sunshine the following morning, many herdsmen arrived. They began pitching their tents, erecting a large one right next to the yogins, and as they did so, they said, "Won't you yogins give us a hand?"

Mila replied, "I never do such mundane work."

A herdsman countered, "Well, aren't eating and drinking mundane work? Or don't you eat, either?"

"I do not know how to eat as you do," Mila replied evenly.

"That is a big lie, yogin," snapped the herdsmen. "So just how *do* you eat?"

In reply, Mila sang this song:

> To great translator Marpa,
> Renowned man of Lho Drak,
> Precious 'father', true lama,
> I pray, grant me blessings.
> I, Yogi-repa of Tibet,
> Offer this from the true natural state:
>
> In this broad meadow of fundamental awareness
> I pitch the tent of unchanging reality.
> I raise the stout tentpole of faith,
> Tie the ropes of mind-for-enlightenment,

Erect the sidepoles of method and wisdom,
Drive in the stakes of the unswerving path,
And raise the banner of mahamudra.

Within this tent of reality
Upon cushions of four infinitudes
Sit I, the divine yogin, in introspection.
I have closed the curtain of unchanging clear light
And embraced the bride of clear production phase,
After hiding the dowry of profound completion phase;
Thus conceiving the infant of clear-light awareness.

I am attended by servants of the ten virtues
As I invest the seven superior treasures
And shepherd the grazing flocks of compassion and voidness.

I eat the food of pure concentration,
Cooked on the stove of the profound path of method,
And drink from the flowing stream of enlightenment.

For clothes I wear the bliss-warmth of tummo
And keep watch for the three enemy poisons,
Fending them off by knowing
What to accept and what to reject.

The stallion of pure supplication
Is harnessed and saddled with method and wisdom;
I, the yogin, ride on him.

Wearing the armor of patience
I drive him on with the whip of vigor.
Holding the weapon of wisdom in hand,
I constantly fight the enemy, the afflictions.

On the long spear of gnosis,
I hoist the banner of special intent;
I have won the victory over samsara.

The herdsman commented, "These are talkative yogins! If you have attained independence, how come you haven't the means to get even one animal hide for a robe?"

Mila replied:

> I pray at the feet of my lama.
>
> You eat the sinful food of flesh and fat;
> I eat nettles and wild leeks.
>
> You drink the sinful draught of dark beer;
> I slake my thirst at cool mountain cascades.
>
> You wear clothes of animal hide;
> I wear the robe of tummo warmth.
>
> You engage yourselves in sinful behavior;
> I devote myself to virtuous deeds.
>
> You will wander samsara's low realms;
> I am headed for the realm of reality.
>
> Without eating the food of concentration,
> How could I endure hunger with no provisions?
>
> If not warmed by the bliss-warmth of tummo,
> How could I survive with a robe of mere cotton?
>
> If not endowed with yogic awareness,
> How could I wander such desolate country?
>
> Without realizing the illusion of the apparent,
> How could I hoist myself up into thin air?
>
> Never before have I lied or deceived,
> I know no reason for doing so.

As he sang these last verses, he elevated himself about ten feet into the air and hovered there, legs crossed. All the herdsmen were then sorry, and offered their respects and apologies. One young man in particular spoke up, "Precious lama, I regret the many sins I committed before this. Permit me to follow in your footsteps, my lama, wherever you lead me."

Realizing that he had unfinished karmic business with this man, Mila allowed him to follow and he eventually became an excellent yogin.

The Dice Players

The Tibetan version of craps is played with a pair of dice bored with holes to indicate the numbers. They are shaken overhead in a leather cup and brought down sharply on the playing board with a shout indicating the number required in one's strategy, and perhaps accompanied by an extemporaneous verse or comment. The play consists of moving markers called dogs *through a long line of pebbles according to each throw. A player may "bump" another player's dog back to the beginning by landing on the place it occupies. The first player to arrive at the end by throwing the exact number required is the winner; the others incur debts according to the number of stones between their dogs and the end. This game still maintains its popularity alongside mah-jongg and chess, sometimes to the detriment of the players' daily affairs, as indicated in the following song.*

One summer the great Jetsun went begging in Tagkar Ngonma in the northern part of Upper Tibet. There he encountered a group of men gathered at a village square playing dice at several tables. A monk in the crowd said to Mila, "Yogin, if you can, sing these dice players a song about the evils of dice. Afterwards I will help you beg."

So Mila complied with this song:

I bow to the feet of my holy lama,
Embodiment of Conqueror Vajradhara,
Who vanquished enemies in three worldly realms:
Bless me to conquer my emotional enemies.

Now listen, patrons gathered here,
I'll sing a song of the evils of dice—
Excuse me if it is too revealing.

The dice board before you,
Is cause of the failure of all your plans;
Arranged with stones tallying the debts of afflictions
And five dogs who carry five emotional poisons.

In the abysmal dice-cup of dark delusion
Rattle the two paired dice of desire and hatred,
Bored with holes like worm-holes in ruined goods.

Shaking these ruiners aloft in hand,
You might as well declare, "I go to low states,"
Instead of proclaiming points needed, and slap the cup down.

As you count the white and black stones of karma,
I say you are ruining all happiness and ease,
Sending yourselves back to low states,
Through many passes and valleys, to miserable lives.

At first it is a ruinous disease of the mind,
Then it leads to depravity and senseless, harsh talk;
It ends in the bad trouble of fights.

Act always with the wholesomeness of the ten virtues
Fleeing far from the evils of such ways.

One of the dice players said jokingly, "Well, yogin, how do *you* play
dice?"
So Mila sang:

I pray to my lama whose kindness
I can never repay: grant me blessings.

On the table of unfaltering faith,
I spread the stones of good and bad action
And aim the eye of the ten good virtues
At the paired dice of method and wisdom
Within the cup of tranquilization experience.

Holding it high in the hand of enlightenment-mind,
I invert it like pure view falling from above,
And crying out a plaintive prayer,
I slap it down like the kiss of close embrace
On the upward-climbing stairway of practice.

Then, tallying stones with analytic wisdom,
I rout the dogs of poisonous emotions
With five wisdom dogs of my own.

Pressing on through passes of stages and paths,
I arrive at the end of the ten-stage journey,
Victorious over the playboard of samsara.

Do you get my meaning, friends?

They were very impressed and questioned Jetsun carefully, asking "Where
are you from?" and so on. Jetsun replied with this song:

I pray to my holy lama.

I will give you answers to your questions:
"Where are you from? Where are you going?"
I come from the bardo land of death.
I am going to higher realms and liberation.
Although I came here as a beggar among you,
I am not begging out of hunger
But to urge you on to virtue
That you may acquire merit.

If you have faith in this, acquire merit.
If you have the means, practice giving.

If you are industrious, practice Dharma.
Well understood, Dharma is more precious than gold;
Misunderstood, it is a thorn in the ear.

May you have the fortune of victory over samsara.

Everyone was inspired with strong faith and requested Dharma instruction. They made offerings, but Mila did not accept them. Some followed him, and it is said that by practicing meditation, many of them gained a foothold on the path.

Song for the Fisher Girls

While the great Jetsun was traveling in the Yardrok region of Tsang province, he came upon a group of women cleaning small fish. He was moved by intense compassion and wept profusely.

One young girl asked him, "Why are you crying yogin? Are you embarrassed at your total lack of clothes?" Mila's reply was in the style of a folk song:

> Great person Marpa Lotsawa,
> Turn your eye of compassion upon us
> From the state of pure reality!
> Guide all beings of the six realms onto the path.
>
> You bloody-mouthed cannibals
> Who kill other beings
> For the sake of a living,
> Listen a moment!
>
> Look all you want
> At my pale yogin's body,
> Weakened by poor food;
> There's not much to understand.
>
> Listen instead to this song
> Flowing from my lips.
> Understand its meaning;
> It will help you in the long run.

Generally speaking, all beings
Have been our parents through beginningless time;
In particular, you yourselves can not bear
Even the pain of a thorn in your flesh!
But you are murdering others for food!
Look! Think! Examine your actions,
Oh hard-hearted women!

These gutted carcasses
Still flip around.
Consider this well!
Think! Try to understand!

Such hard-hearted women,
Are your hearts made of stone?
Or are they hard iron?
There is no certainty to life,
No assurance we will be here tomorrow.
When mind and body separate
And your consciousness takes rebirth
In the hell of unceasing torment,
A mass of weapons will fall
Like rain on your body,
Trapped on a plain of hot burning iron.

Such immense misery
Is impossible to describe!

Only the movement of in and out breath
Separates this life from the next;
Beyond this there is nothing.
When the movement of breath stops,
You'll surely experience the results of bad action.

The only consolation in this
Is the elimination of all evil,
So apply yourselves to Dharma.

This song I sing
May offend your ears,
But in the long run
May it spur you to practice.

The women were deeply moved. Circling him, they offered their respects. They admitted their previous evil behavior and resolved firmly to stop it. It is said that some of them went on to practice Dharma and became accomplished meditators.

Song for an Old Woman

While traveling toward Nya Nang, the great Jetsun stopped at a cliff cave at the border of the province and got ready to sleep. An old woman approached him and said defensively, "Don't sleep here; you might rob me!" The Jetsun, moved by strong compassion, sang this song in response:

To my kind lama with Holy body
I pray, grant me blessings.

Hair white, but neglectful of Dharma,
Forehead wrinkled, but still longing for sex,
Toothless, but bound with attachment,
Body bent, but clinging tightly to self,
Listen to me, lady of low thoughts.

First, the paths to high birth and freedom,
Second, the abyss of low birth and samsara,
Third, the bardo, without choice of rebirth;
Enmeshed in these three,
Hoarded possessions are enjoyed by others,
But the baggage of ripe sins is borne by yourself.

Abandoned in darkness, nowhere to go,
Lady intent on contending with Dharma,
Consider your own thoughts!

Watch your own mind!
Think! Observe your body!
Examine! Understand former actions!

First, cooking food morning and evening,
Second, affairs left undone,
Third, social formalities for insatiable friends;
Enmeshed in these three,
Ignoring all memory of previous deeds,
You later create the cause for dispute.

When abandoned in bardo, knowing not what to do,
Lady intent on harming yourself,
Consider your own thoughts!
Watch your mind!
Think! Observe friends insatiable!
Examine! Understand relations with others!

First, bathing daughter-in-law's son,
Second, criticized by your son,
Third, disruption by wild-headed grandchildren;
Enmeshed in these three,
You're deeply distracted when practicing Dharma
And fear censure by men in relations with others;
A great fire of resentment burns deep within you.

Unlucky lady, failing in strength,
Consider your own thoughts!
Watch your mind!
Think! Understand former actions!
Examine! Observe your condition!

First, age-wrinkled skin outside,
Second, flesh and bloodless bones inside,
Third, in between, senses fail—deaf and blind—
Enmeshed in these three,
Though you seem happy, your legs tremble and shake,

You try to stand straight, but your neck muscles fail,
You try to maintain, but voice and body grow useless.

Pitiful lady of failing health,
Consider your own thoughts!
Watch your mind!
Think! Understand former actions!
Examine! Observe your condition!

High birth conditions: more scarce than a star in daylight.
Low birth conditions: more popular than fresh meat.
Meanwhile, plagued by a preta's neuroses,
Enmeshed as you are in these three,
Consider your thoughts!
Watch your mind!
Think! Understand former actions!
Examine! Observe your condition!
Oh lady, beware of such things!

Struck with regret upon hearing this song, the woman offered her apology and, by requesting Dharma instruction, entered the path.

Mila in the Boondocks

After staying awhile in the mountain caves near Nyam Nying, Mila ventured into a primitive region where many different dialects were spoken. Here he stayed in a yoga cave for one month, teaching Dharma to many elemental spirits. When he went in search of human students who could be vessels for the teachings, he discovered that the people were more like animals than humans. In a state of depression, he sang this song:

I bow to the feet of Dharma lord, teacher Marpa,
Lotsawa who removes the darkness of ignorance.

In the dark gloom of this barbaric place,
Unlit by the sun of holy Dharma,
The people have human bodies,
But the workings of their minds
Preclude interest in any pursuit
Save eating, drinking and pleasure.

Hear this song of my depression
Nonhumans, gods and spirits:
Through prior action they have inferior lives,
And in such inferior lives again and again
They take low rebirth through bad actions.
Seeing these human bodies with animal minds
I myself became depressed in mind.

Compassion wells up from the depths of my heart
But I'm unable to be of any help.

May they all be my trainees
When I've advanced to enlightenment.

You local gods and your attendants
Dwelling in these yoga caves—
Strive to further their struggle towards light!

So he traveled through this land of many dialects seeking students, but most people ran away at the sight of the great Jetsun. However, he established karmic connection with these frightened people by meditating on great love and making sincere supplication for them.

He then arrived in Lower Tsum only to discover this area was no better. Thinking to increase his mental powers by finding a cave conducive to practice, and hoping to establish Dharma connections with these barbarians, he went searching across the mountainsides. Arriving at the cave of a wealthy pigeon, he found the bird standing next to a bushel-sized pile of rice. She gestured to Jetsun by nodding her head.

"Are you giving this to me?" he asked.

She replied by nodding her head. Jetsun thought, "In these barbaric lands the animals are more considerate than people!" So he sang this song:

I pray at the feet of my father-lama.
To return your kindness, skillful one,
I illumined my mind with all realizations.

Many superficial, illusory appearances
Have been reflected in the mirror of my mind.
This old man has come a long way—
He's seen amazing sights,
Heard incredible things,
Tasted strange-tasting foods,
And felt intense sorrow for his 'relatives' in the six realms.

I met with a rich patron-pigeon
Who in faith gave me wild white rice—
If I told this to others, they would call it a lie.
Such things seldom happen to others;
Yet, it is so amazing I had to speak of it.

I, Venerable Milarepa,
Share this from the realm of great bliss.
I make impartial supplication,
Good wishes from the realm of true being.

Accept this song of worship, holy lama.
Share this music, host of dakinis.
Remove your obstructions, nonhumans.

He took the rice and stayed for three months in a cave high above the land. When he was ready to leave, he prayed:

Having received white, wild rice
From a patron-pigeon
The venerable Milarepa
Practiced for three months.

By virtue of this merit the pigeon gained,
May she be freed from her animal state.
After winning a body of leisure and opportunity,
With all the advantages of higher life,
May she unfold the wings of method and wisdom
And soar into the sky of true being.

May she finally experience resultant
Endowment with the four bodies and five gnoses
In the palace of Akanishta Heaven.

Then Mila continued northward, to Upper Tsum. There he met a woman who asked, "Where did you come from?"

"I have just now come from below. I have no plan to go further than this," he replied.

She said, "Last night I had an auspicious dream, so today I will stay here." So she stayed, and the following morning she said, "If you are going to seek alms, I will help you."

Thereupon, Mila sang this song:

I pray to all lamas, and in particular
Take refuge in my own kind lama.

I am a yogin who wanders the countryside,
A beggar who travels alone,
A pauper who has nothing.
Moved by this, you spoke up,
So listen now, faithful woman:

I left the land of my birth behind,
Turned my back on my own fine house,
And gave up my fertile fields.

I stayed in isolated mountain retreats,
Practiced in rock caves surrounded by snow,
And found food as birds do;
That is how it has been up to now.

There is no telling the day of my death,
But I have a purpose before I die.
That's the story of me, the yogin.
Now I will give you some advice.

Trying to control the events of this life,
Trying and trying to be so clever,
Always planning to manipulate your world,
Involved in repetitive social relations;
In the midst of these plans for the future,
You arrive, unaware, at your final years.
Not realizing your brow is knit with wrinkles,
Not knowing your hair has turned to white,
Not seeing the skin of your eyes sink down,
Not admitting the sag of your mouth and nose.

Even while chased by the envoys of death,
You still sing and rejoice in pleasure.
Not knowing if life will last till morning,

You still make plans for tomorrow's future.
Not knowing in which realm rebirth will occur,
You are still content and complacent.

Now is the time to get ready for death—
That is my sincere advice to you:
If its import strikes you, start your practice.

With strong faith she gave him one month's provisions, and after receiving Dharma, gained a foothold on the path.

Song of Escort

Mila was staying at Red Block Rock and had just concluded a teaching for several young repas. His students told him, "Ten days from now some of us will go begging, some will wander the mountains, some will travel around the country, and some will visit the Lion Cave of Paro Tagtsang.[7] Please consider giving us a farewell song." So Mila sang:

Father lama, pray grant me blessings.

You repas seated in order
With Tön and Shengom at the head,
And at the rear "Tön the Bearded,"
And the assiduous Rechungpa,
Have all asked me for a teaching;
To that end I will tell you this:

If you listen to this old man you will be wise.
If you observe a bird's flight you will understand timing.
If you measure your bravery your life will be secure.
If your mind is expansive you will be in harmony with all.
If you're moderate in eating you will be healthy.

Now I will explain the essential meaning
Implied in these examples:

You say that after one, two, three, or ten days
Some will go begging,
Some will wander in the mountains,

And some will wander around the country. . . .
Whatever it is, listen to me.

If you act in accord with Dharma you are wise.
If your compassionate method is strong it will benefit others.
If you realize wise vision it will benefit yourselves.
If you integrate wisdom and method it will benefit everyone.

I, Mila, have some precepts for you,
So hear these words with attentive ear;
Bear their meaning, unforgotten, deep in your heart.

Though you have ". . . listened to profound Dharma
At the feet of an excellent father-lama,"
If you have not penetrated mind's conceptual workings
Do not give empty, mindless teachings
While wandering aimlessly around the country;
There is danger in the results of such bad action.

Until you have firm conviction in cause and effect,
Do not turn the heads of devotees
With seemingly good but pretentious behavior
Out of desire for wealth and fame;
There is danger in the massed results of such wrong
    livelihood.

Until you know the one corrective antidote
Which, when realized, yields skill in everything,
Do not repeat the wrathful mantras "Hum" and "Phat"
In the desolate mountains of demon country;
There is danger they will obstruct your practice.

Though you've the four empowerments of the developmental
    process,
Unless you have *real* skill
In containing bindu,
Don't take on a human yogic consort;[8]
There is danger of birth in the vajra-hells.

Although you have performed services of worship,
Unless you regard even enemies of the teachings
With a mind of great compassion,
Do not use powers and forceful mantras
On behalf of your own problems and pleasures;
There is danger of rebirth as a carnivore.

Though you have the currents under mental control,
Do not harass others
By showing wild animal forms
Through miraculous emanations;
There is danger of rebirth as a graveyard ghoul.

This short experience-song with six prohibitions
By me, the yogin Milarepa,
Expresses in song my precepts
For you, disciple-offspring.

May this be an offering for those who seek alms,
A companion for those who wander the mountains,
Provision for those who travel the countryside,
And a sight for those who seek visions.

May it be a reception for those who arrive,
Company for those who stay,
And an escort for those who go.

May all of you—arriving, staying, or going—
Have utmost happiness and bliss in this life.
May obstructions in practice be removed,
Help for beings spontaneously provided
By integration of method and wisdom,
And nirvana be attained for yourselves and others.

This was the song with six prohibitions.

PART TWO

PATH SONGS

Basic Teachings

People turn to religion for one of three reasons: some want to improve their lot in life and relieve their fear of death. Others, wanting to escape the inevitable pain of life, extinguish *all* aspects of life through attainment of nirvana. And some, understanding the interconnectedness of all life, seek to free all beings from the bondage of illusion. Although this latter type, the bodhisattva, is afforded the highest respect in the Great Vehicle System (Mahayana) of Buddhism, the first two types of spiritual practitioners are not disparaged. The efforts of people of the first type, initially aimed at self-improvement, may eventually result in a maturity of mind that enables them to consider the welfare of others. For those of the second type, who are unable to cope with the misery of life, the refuge of their personal nirvana is not final—it is a temporary respite from suffering which may also eventually lead to the maturity of the bodhisattva's realization of universal responsibility.

As a champion of the bodhisattva ideal, Mila's best teachings deal with practices of a bodhisattva. But because he taught from personal experience of the human condition, he always fashioned his teachings according to his audience. To simple folk concerned with worldly matters he gave basic teachings about action and its results (karma), the inevitable misery of the conditioned mind, and the benefits of right action. His description of the tortures of lower states in "The Ups and Downs of Samsara" is meant to prod his audience out of its complacency and make use of this precious human existence for spiritual advancement. It is not pessimism, but a statement of fact: the pain of life is the basic condition and ground of the path to freedom.

The term *path* refers to the course and elements of spiritual development (described in the introduction to *Drinking the Mountain Stream*). Although Mila describes the correct path as "sure," meaning that its validity is self-evident, it is not an established thoroughfare, but is created dynamically by the practitioner himself. Not only does the appropriate practice differ according to the personality of the practitioner, it also changes during the course of development. The pace of development and the points where the strategy of practice must be altered depend on the individual's basic nature, ability, experience, and determination. In "Mila Teaches Two Scholars How to Practice," Mila describes how his teacher Marpa denied him formal instruction until he removed the obstructions to development resulting

51

from his earlier experiences and actions. To accomplish this, Marpa gave him the work of constructing and tearing down several buildings, which took several years and caused Mila much pain and physical injury. Mila's case was extreme, because his early experiences had left him with a large burden of negative attitudes and conditionings. For the two scholars, however, the removal of obstacles had been accomplished by arduous study of scripture, philosophy, and logic. Although Mila usually disparaged such scholarly pursuits, on this occasion he says, "Your prior studies have prepared you well." Knowledge gained from formal study and reflection on scriptural teachings can be a valuable prerequisite to meditation practice. However it is achieved, a thorough intellectual understanding of the mind and the world is prerequisite to advanced meditation. This story is an excellent exposition of the stages of meditative practice, from basic concentration to advanced techniques such as mahamudra, by which the very foundations of the egoistic, conceptualizing mind are shaken.

A teacher (lama) is someone who provides the inspiration to apply a practice or understand a truth. He cannot hand out insight, but through personal experience he can make traditional teachings meaningful for each student, help "tune up" their practice, and correct mistakes with helpful tips. "Rechungpa's Pride" is a good example of this process. The intensity of Rechungpa's first taste of the experience of voidness made him think he had achieved ultimate realization. Words would not have convinced him of his error, so Mila gave a direct demonstration of his superior powers, a lesson perfectly suited to Rechungpa's self-assured and prideful personality. This song is also an example of Milarepa's frequent warning to advanced students that the bliss experienced in the course of meditative practice must not be mistaken for ultimate realization. A breakthrough in the course of practice can be overwhelming; thus, an experienced teacher is needed to show that it is only a step in the right direction. The frequently used expression "spontaneous freedom" refers to the *nature* of true freedom, not the manner in which it is attained. "Spontaneous" freedom occurs after deliberate practice resulting in a gradual progression of experiences which, when correctly understood, leads to ultimate realization.

The path is made accessible here-and-now by living teachers, but its integrity is preserved through the ages by tradition and ritual. The underlying magnetism of ritual imbues it with the power to focus practice. Tradition and essence—form and content—are inseparable; problems arise only when one is overemphasized. The fault of valuing form over content is illustrated in "Mila Teaches a Famous Lama about the Real and the Apparent." A prestigious lama is making a ritual offering to a lake-dwelling naga (serpent or dragon), a native Tibetan practice which predates buddhism. But the naga values Mila's offer of a tiny herbal pill more than the lama's extravagant gifts. When questioned, Mila explains that the value of an offering resides not in the gift, but in the attitude and intent of the giving. Likewise, ritual and mental attitude must function together. The ultimate ritual of offering the unofferable—to make a gift of the universe itself—requires a truly expansive mind.

Mila Teaches a Famous Lama about the Real and the Apparent

Once a lama of Ja Mongpo,[9] who was reputed to be a siddha, went to Lake Lhatso-Sintso to make offerings and seek the blessing of the naga living there. He dropped many medicines, food, and precious things such as gold, silver, and bolts of brocade, cotton, and silk, into the lake. He had also brought along many lama-scholars[10] to add their spiritual energy to the dedication of offerings. The serpent of the lake surfaced, and the lama asked her, "Is this enough wealth, food and drink for you?"

The serpent replied, "It is enough, but on the south shore of this lake an even greater offering is being made. I might miss out on it, so please say your prayers quickly."

The lama asked, "If I send someone to the south shore, would he be able to see this offering?"

"If you send a fast horseman at once he could see it."

So the lama sent a man on a fast horse to go look. The naga pointed the way. Meanwhile, on a cliff to the south of Pelmo Plain, Jetsun Milarepa and one of his disciples had placed a small pellet of barley concentrate the size of rat's dung into a clay pot, poured water over it, and were sitting with eyes half-closed. The horseman found them, and after paying his respects and asking for blessings, asked, "Precious Lama, how long will you stay here?"

"I will stay here about seven days," Mila replied.

"Then where will you go?"

"I'll go to a desolate valley called Lachi."

The man made one final bow and went back to make a detailed report to the lama of Ja Mongpo. On the fifth day, guided by the horseman, the lama set out with four disciples and a cow. Upon meeting Jetsun and his disciple, he made a circular feast offering, and afterwards they conversed about Dharma. The lama of Ja Mongpo said, "I dropped many kinds of valuables, food, and drink into Lake Lhatso-Sintso and brought many monks to dedicate the offerings. But the serpent of the lake came and said that a better and greater offering was being made elsewhere. I sent a man to find out, and he reported that he found you, great Jetsun, sitting with eyes half-closed. He said you had poured water into a clay pot containing barley concentrate the size of rat's dung. Please tell me, in a practical sense, which is more important: the offering itself or the mental aim with which it is made?"

In reply, Jetsun sang this song:

Respectful homage with body, speech, and mind
To the lotus feet of great Lord Marpa,
Who creates emanations for the welfare of beings,
Unswayed from the state of reality.
Listen to me, great skillful lama
Possessing the keys of the space-treasury of wisdom.

All superficial phenomena, sights and sounds,
When considered from the viewpoint of the path,
Appear, yet are void; are void, yet appear.

From the viewpoint of unifying appearances and voidness,
Offerings like torma, though great,
Have little power to help you realize the actual state
If your mind has not experienced natural reality.

If, for example, you meditate on superb food and drink,
It will not help relieve the hunger and thirst
Of beings who're starving and thirsty;
Only the real taste of food and drink will.

Likewise, mere knowledge of the natural state
Obtained through analytic wisdom is not enough;
It must be actually realized and experienced.

If you have such realization and experience,
Mental aim free of habitual concepts,[11] along with
A small token, is most important.
Your offerings, though so fine,
Were still made with slight conceptual habits.

Root virtues tainted by poisons and eight worldly concerns[12]
Are the general cause of samsaric existence.
All mundane virtue and evil,
Though void of identity in themselves,
Naturally yield their dependently arising
Good and bad karmic results
Due to their dependently occurrent nature.

Therefore, any offering, large or small,
Must be sealed with wisdom view
By correctly understanding the way things are.

Thus, the Tibetan Yogin Milarepa
Offers you, great skillful Ja Tön,
His realization as far as he has seen it.
If I made any mistake, I truly apologize.

Lama Ja Tön knelt and paid respects, asking, "Would you please say a bit about the gradual process of the three principles of the path?" So Jetsun sang again:

Respectful homage with body, speech, and mind
To the Dharma-intellect of Teacher Marpa,
Translator endowed with mastery
Of the space-treasury of holy Dharma.

This is my understanding,
Gained from the nectar of his speech:

Special moral practice consists chiefly
Of the seven vows for personal liberation
Observed with body and speech.

These prevent the occurrence
Of evils, both prohibited and natural.[13]

Special mental practice,
Which is to be universally directed,
Is chiefly of the Great Vehicle.[14]

Special wisdom practice,
Like the former, must be universal,
And focuses mainly on reality
Through analysis aimed at the real, natural state.

To explain these special practices in detail
Would take awhile; for now
I have merely indicated their essentials.

Again the lama of Ja Mongpo asked:

Holy yogin practicing austerities
Wearing such a strange cotton robe,
Bare body endowed with brilliance,
I bow to the feet of this Buddha-repa.

You have answered my question, yogin.
Now, by your great mercy,
Please untangle the knot of my doubts
And explain a bit more
About the gradual process
Of the special practices of mind and wisdom.

So again Mila sang:

I bow to the feet of Translator Marpa
Who revealed the essence of the natural state.

From the basis process,
Through ignorant action,
The other processes arise.[15]

Among them, the conscious process
Is called *mind*.

The functioning of mind is universal
And can cognize all eighty-four thousand
Afflictive mental functions.

By controlling the mind alone,
All afflictions are controlled.
Thus, the skillful way of learning
The special practice of mind is to realize
First, that mind has no source;
Next, mind has no locus;
And finally, mind has no essence.

It is produced and stopped each moment.
If pushed, it will not go;
If drawn closer, it will not stay.
It has no shape or color whatsoever.

Mundane, illusory samsara, though nonexistent,
Arises through the power of illusion.
Previously you did not understand this pattern,
So now I have explained it to you.
Belief in the reality of illusory appearances is the universal
    mistake;
You must analyze and meditate with this understanding.

Examine this thoroughly
Under the guidance of a wise, realized lama,
Who is compassionate and skilled in method.
Then, in an isolated no-man's land,
Meditate diligently, heedless of comfort or death,
Until you have obtained the essence of the natural state.

As you become practiced in this,
Work for others' welfare with body, speech, and mind,

Your mind aimed at supreme enlightenment,
And motivated by infinite compassion
For all beings who are not so realized,
For the sake of their realization.

Abandon all nonconducive faults
And cultivate all conducive virtues.
Such constant, consistent cultivation,
Imbued with alertness, memory, and awareness,
Is called *special mental practice*.

In the special practice of wisdom
Three things are of great importance:
Constant cultivation of certitude
Through the wisdoms of learning and reflection,
Continual nurturing of the assets
Gained from scripture and realization,
And the developmental signs of realization.

Here is the method of focusing mind in the natural state—
Examine and analyze it with penetrating intellect.
Whatever causes and circumstances occur—
Only those phenomena arise.
They are neither existent nor nonexistent,
Free of duality, void of identity.

They are not void,
They are not nonvoid,
Nor are they both void and nonvoid.

The son of a barren woman
Ties a sky-flower to his head,
Holds a hare's long horn in hand,
And views dream companions as real.

He who speaks such words
Has attained the state of reality;
About reality itself, nothing can be said.

The lama of Ja Mongpo knelt respectfully with folded hands and sang:

Oh, precious, supreme being,
Though I heard your name before,
Admiration failed to dawn in my mind.

I came before you to ask
The difference between material object and mental aim;
You clearly explained the difference
And I understood something of what is and what is not.

Thank you, precious Mila!
You are endowed with compassion, yogin!
Great wonder, best of siddhas!

He made generous offerings, but Mila rejected them, singing:

I bow to the feet of Translator Marpa,
Father with mastery of the space-treasury of Dharma.

First, develop the wisdoms of learning and reflection.
Next, meditate one-pointedly on the object we thus
    determined.
Finally, you will gain the fruits of meditation.

Listen, "siddha" striving for the natural state:
A beautiful, white snow-mountain
Is enfolded in sunbeams and illuminated,
As the mountain of your basis process
Was illuminated by the sunbeams of my precepts.

It is a great mistake to conduct meditation
Aimed at realizing the actual state *as an object*
By examining the intentions of sutra and shastra,
With the wisdoms of learning and reflection.

It is also a great mistake to remain in
And consider to be ultimate the bliss, clarity, freedom from
    thought,

And the apparent experiences of tranquilization,
Which merely signal developmental stages in cultivating
    experience.

Well then, how is it done?
Afflictions are completely conquered
By insight imbued with tranquilization.
By analytic wisdom aimed at the natural state,
Analytic awareness and voidness
Are focused in the unwavering state.

With good experiences and realization,
The fast horse is ridden onward.
When the heart of the natural state is reached,
You will be liberated from subject-object duality.

Then, when superficial reality is confronted,
Appearances are still distinct, but no longer concrete.
These dreamlike, illusory appearances
Become forms holding no significance,
Inert, without content,
Totally unobstructive to penetration.

When reality is attained,
One who has experienced the objective,
The inexpressible, inconceivable Mother of Conquerors,
Deserves the title "siddha."

Those endowed with mind-for-enlightenment
And motivated by infinite compassion
Should integrate method and wisdom for the sake
Of liberating beings who lack this realization
From their wanderings in samsara.

Afterwards, Jetsun and his disciple went to Chu Bar. This was the story
of Lake Lhatso-Sintso, where Mila taught the lama about the real and the
apparent.

61

Rechungpa's Pride

Once while Jetsun was staying in the Lower-Hollow Cave of Lachi, he gave his spiritual son Rechung Dorje Dragpa the instructions for generating spontaneous mahamudra. When Rechungpa had actually achieved a state of realization he remained in clear voidness for a long time. Arising from this concentration, he thought, "This is the spontaneous natural state of mind! Does my lama have any realization greater than this?"

He went to Milarepa but before he could ask anything, Mila said, "Son, Rechungpa, such ease in cultivating meditation and quick experience of awareness in a youthful beginner indicates your heritage of personal power of merit compiled in former lives. Now your thought upon concluding your first morning session—'Does my lama have any realization greater than this?'—is an act of pride. You should confess it; otherwise, it will obstruct your meditation. Understand and bear in mind that it was your old spiritual father who explained the fine points of meditation, thus clarifying the objective of that realization you experienced." He then sang this song about the recognition of spontaneous freedom:

> I bow to the feet of Translator Marpa, best of men,
> Working for beings' welfare with manifold emanations,
> Though not distracted from the state of pure reality
> Within the reality-realm of great bliss.
> Grant your blessings of realization and experience
> To me and all my followers.
>
> Son, Rechungpa, listen well.
> Consider carefully, Dorje Drak.
> Examine thoroughly, young cotton-clad friend.

The first step in following
The profound, graduated path to buddhahood
Is to reflect on the difficulty of finding
The leisure and opportunity of human life
And to understand that human life is mere existence.

Then consider death and impermanence;
Reflect in your heart the uncertain time of death.
After that, consider the ills of actions and their results;
Understand well the virtues and evils you have created.

Lama and Triple Gem are the sole refuge.
For protection from lower states
Due to the force of evil deeds,
There is no refuge other than these.
Take refuge, acquire virtue, expiate evil,
And offer the seven-fold service[16] of worship.

Without finding the goal, the natural state,
You will escape to the freedom
Which is beyond the highs and lows of samsara.

If you wish to see the goal of reality,
Purify previous obstructive evils with the hundred-syllable
    mantra
And accumulate the two stores with mandala offerings, and so
    on.[17]

Then, after merging your mind with the Lama's
Through intense, longing prayer
To your kind root lama and his lineage,[18]
Practice the graded instructions for tranquilization.
Progress from mere inception of stability
Onward in gradual steps.

Because the natural state is the root,
It looks so easy, yet is very hard.

But when awareness is focused on reality
After intellectual analysis has been carried out
By learning and reflecting,
This one realization totally liberates.
It looks so hard, yet is very easy.

Thus it is vital to attend
A skillful lama possessed of experience.
Your recent meditation experience
Caused you to think: "Does my lama
Have realization greater than this?"
Son, this was due to insufficient learning.

If realization does not need refinement
Beyond this point,
The many scriptures which
Open the doors to diverse concentrations
Would all be senseless blather.

The gradual process of paths and stages
Is like gaining fluency in a language:
How could mere knowledge of the first letter
Be considered complete skill in reading?

If you wish to acquire reading skills,
First learn the alphabet, letter by letter.
Likewise, if you wish to obtain omniscience,
You must practice both tranquilization and insight
After striving to acquire virtue and expiate evils
Through the process of learning, reflecting, and then
    meditating.

Your recent realization
Was just the tip of tranquilization experience;
It is identified like this:

Mental stabilization without the least wavering
Through the suppression of manifold conceptual patternings,

Is called *tranquilization*.
When classified, there are several types:

Your recent concentration
Was "tranquilization manifesting lucidity,"
Directly based on mental stabilization.
But other levels of refinement exist.

Nowadays, most 'expert meditators'
Consider mental stability to be tranquilization,
And lucidity and clarity to be insight.
This is mere fool's nonsense.

The clarity, energy, distinctness,
Brilliance, purity, and radiance
Of the unwavering, thought-free tranquilization state
Are simply the natural lucidity of tranquilization.

Upon such good stabilization
Collect the nectar of explicit scriptures.
Then explore by learning and reflection
The profound meaning personally taught
By a realized, experienced lama.
Taking up practice as long as life lasts,
Combine analytic and focusing meditations.

Integrate compassion and voidness.
Thus, with mind aimed at enlightenment for the sake of all
    beings,
And with the gnosis that has no fixed objective,
Mount the horse of good supplication.

You will complete the developmental signs of the path
With the strengths of thorough realization,
Knowledge of the keys to meditation,
And cultivation of the gradual path process
With is continuous, like a river's current.

Realizations will then gradually occur and
Superficial appearances can be seen as dream illusions.
Dependent occurrence will be seen as samsara's inner
    workings,
And illusory appearances will be baseless, rootless.

You will know that beings are inseparable from buddhas,
That not even the names "samsara" or "nirvana" exist.
This comprehension of the natural condition,
The actual state, is called *understanding*.

The various events in one-pointed concentration
Are meditation experiences;
When they lead to confrontation with the goal,
That is realization.
When realization free from identity patterning is achieved,
I will show you what it is like:

Striking empty space with his fist, Mila made a ringing sound. Then, striking a rock with his hand, he left a clear handprint as if in moist clay, which is said to exist even to this day.

Rechungpa placed his mind in the "natural condition" as he had previously experienced it and struck a rock with his hand, producing nothing but pain. He then bowed many times and, overcome with intense respect and admiration, he knelt with folded hands and sang:

Homage and praise to the emanation-body
Of my precious Jetsun lama
Endowed with great mercy
And the kindness to guide all beings.

I, Rechung Dorje Dragpa,
Have met with you, lord of beings,
On the strength of a little merit from previous lives.

Mercifully, you taught me holy dharma:
The stage of profound instruction

And the complete instructions for the preparatory practices
Which clear obstructions, compile the stores, and so on.

When I produced a little stabilization
While striving for the basic state of tranquilization and
    insight,
I thought it was the end of meditation
And thus was proud and conceited.

You read these thoughts in the mind
Of one so weak and inexperienced as myself,
And, by the catapult of your blessed speech,
Toppled me from the treetop of my pride.

You drew me from the depths of my pool of conceit,
And cleared my deluded fog of ignorance
With the sunshine of merciful compassion,
Opening the lotus-petals of my confused mind.

I have no way of returning your kindness
For acquainting me with mind's actual state.
So, to repay you for guiding me with compassion,
I offer you body, speech, and mind;
I will take up practice as you command.

Look on me with wisdom, compassionate one!
Protect me with kindness, merciful one!
And like a body and its shadow,
May I always be close to you.

Then the great Jetsun spoke: "Well, my son Rechungpa, living beings of the six realms, afflicted with the sickness of ignorance and attached to illusory appearances, have been bewildered throughout beginningless samsara. They take what is selfless to be a self, what is egoless to be an ego; thus, they are adrift on the ocean of samsaric misery with its automatic activation of the imprintings of evil action.

"Now I will explain the inner workings of this. Beings wander in samsara due to the activity of the twelve causal links of dependent occurrence. First, ignorance—that is not knowing, understanding, or realizing the actual condition of the objects and events of our experience—provides the condition for the synthesis of the elements of samsaric existence. This process encompasses the inevitable miseries of birth, sickness, aging, and death.

"This process can be corrected by first understanding the difficulty of obtaining the leisure and opportunity of well-endowed human life, then seeing that such leisure and opportunity, found only once in a hundred births, are impermanent, and finally realizing that the time of death is uncertain. You must reflect on the fact that you will never know where you will be reborn after dying. Because we are inexorably impelled by the force of action, you must consider the cause-effect relationship of action.

"The majority of beings take lower rebirths through the force of bad actions. Such lower states are miserable, and even lives in the higher states are by nature miserable. You must consider in detail the general and specific faults of samsara.

"The special refuge for protection from this is the Triple Gem: the precious, perfect Buddha who is able to guide others through his own freedom from samsara; his precious teachings—the holy dharma of scripture, realization, cessation of misery, and the path to such cessation; and the precious community of great warrior bodhisattvas. They have, by relying on the first two Gems, attained the high position of working for the welfare of beings with the mind aimed at supreme enlightenment, accepting the heavy burden of freeing all beings.

"At the core of the Triple Gem is the kind lama himself. He is the teacher of the holy Dharma, the navigator for freedom from samsara, the guide who leads us to the garden of liberation, the doctor who cures the sickness of the three poisons, the medicine which dissolves the cataracts of ignorance in our eyes, the mirror which clearly reveals what is favorable and unfavorable for development, the wish-fulfilling gem which quickly grants all siddhis—ordinary and supreme. In particular he is the peerless friend who has shown us much kindness." Mila then sang:

> Lama is buddha, lama is dharma,
> And likewise, lama is holy community.
> Lama is the root of everything.

Great master Naropa said:
"Before the advent of the lama
Not even the name *buddha* existed."
Even the host of deities of a thousand eons
Depend on these lamas.

Throughout all authentic scripture
The lama is said to embody the Triple Gem.

"Thus," Mila continued, "taking refuge with confidence in lama and Triple Gem is the foundation of all Dharma.

"Then, having conceived of samsara as a prison, understand that all beings lost in it are none other than our own parents who have given us birth throughout beginningless time. With love and compassion for those lost in samsara, generate a mind aimed at supreme enlightenment for the sake of their liberation.

"Then ride the great wave of practices aimed at enlightenment: the three basic path practices,[19] the four social means, and the six transcendences; thus, compiling the two stores and removing the two obscurations.[20]

"Specifically concerning the six transcendences: giving, moral behavior, and patience are the means of compiling the store of merit. Concentration and wisdom are the means of compiling the store of gnosis. Vigor furthers all of them. The highest gnosis is the very mind of buddha. Those wishing to obtain it should apply themselves to these various methods.

"After initially taking refuge, under the guidance of a qualified lama, disciples who are vessels of the teaching should generate the mind aimed at enlightenment and compile the stores of merit and gnosis by offering the seven-fold service and by practicing guru yoga, mandala offerings, prayers, and so on. They should strive to clear away the blockages of previous bad actions with meditation and repetition of the hundred-syllable Vajrasattva mantra.

"It is of the utmost importance to persevere in all this for months and even years until the signs of development occur. Even after such signs and indications have occurred, you must still achieve spontaneous concentration by the gradual process of realizational states supported by the store of previously compiled merit.

"In general, beginners achieve mental stability by degrees: their stream of thought at first breaks through like a mountain cascade, but eventually the mind remains focused wherever it is placed. This is called *mental stability*. Because it is the foundation of the absorption levels, there is no advancement without it. In this state the condition of being blankly absorbed in freedom from thought is called *obscured tranquilization*. In such a condition the various degrees of excitation and depression, coupled with mental discursiveness, will occur.[21]

"The qualities of distinctness, radiance, nakedness, purity, clarity, and lucidity in the state of natural focusing of mind wherever it is placed are simply the natural lucidity of tranquilization. Some "expert meditators" identify this natural focusing of mind free from thought as tranquilization, and the mental clarity and lucidity of that state as insight. Such people do not understand the necessary distinction between concentration and wisdom.

"What is this distinction? I already explained concentration, which involves tranquilization. Wisdom, which involves insight, is developed as follows:

"*Focusing meditation* is analytic meditation which repeatedly examines the mistaken assumptions involved in learning and reflecting on the teachings of an experienced, skillful lama concerning the explicit import of the scriptures. It must be firmly combined with the previously developed tranquilization concentration. The explicit goal of such analysis is the *understanding* of the actual condition of things. The various mental events and apparitional experiences occurring in the mind which is equipoised in such correct understanding and is firmly based in tranquilization are *developmental experiences*. Supported by these experiences, the direct confrontation with the goal, the natural state, is *realization*.

"In brief, the basis is faith, the assistant is vigor, the antidote is the acquisition of virtue and the expiation of evil, the direct cause is the integration of wisdom with method, and the subsidiary cause is the practice of the accumulation and application paths. When the path of seeing is thereby attained, that is the direct experience of insight wisdom. This is what excellent Marpa taught. The processes of the path of seeing and of the meditation path, as well as those of instantaneous mahamudra, I will explain to you, son, in the course of your development." Mila then sang:

I bow to the feet of Marpa, best of men,
The sight of whose body inspires faith,
Whose voice is sweet to hear,
Whose mind is absorbed in nonperception of identities.

I bow to your feet, Translator Marpa,
Peerless holy man of Lho Drak,
Consistently kind teacher Marpa,
Lotsawa endowed with compassion.

I bow to your feet, speaker of two tongues,
Endowed with the eye of omniscient gnosis,
Mercifully compassionate one
With the ability to grant refuge.

I and all my disciples,
Followers of your lineage of practice,
Yearn for your gift of blessings for realization.
Pray look after us with the eye of gnosis,
Father, from your palace of pure reality,
Pray visit us on feet of miracles.

Bless our bodies with your body.
Bless our speech with your speech.
Bless our minds with your mind.
Grant us your continual blessings.

This eulogy induced realization in Rechungpa's mind which exceeded his previous one. He intensified his efforts in practice and is said to have experienced unusual realization.

Mila Teaches Two Scholars How to Practice

Once when the great Jetsun was staying at Horse-hoof Rock on the slopes of the Indestructible Rock Mountain, two lama-scholars (geshés) of natural science and philosophy arrived. One said to him, "We came here after hearing of the reputation of the great Jetsun. We have pursued the study of natural science and philosophy in the past, but are merely able to give academic answers to questions about transcendent wisdom and epistemology.[22] Now we wish to further our spiritual knowledge by practicing meditation. Jetsun Lama, what is the name of your birthplace? What have you studied?"

Jetsun sat up straight, and, with the blazing brilliance of his powerful intellect, sang this song in the voice of the natural vajra sound:

> I bow to the feet of my true lama
> Who works for beings' welfare with many methods,
> Sending his emanation-body wherever trainees are
> While still abiding in unchanging reality-body.
>
> Listen, you two scholars
> Headed for the goal of the unmistaken path
> Through correct verification
> Of the particular and universal characteristics,[23]
> Which are the patterns of existence—of all things.

You ask me to tell you my life's story.
My ancestral home is Ji Kyiba,
My ancestor, Dodön Senge.
My family moved to Tsa of Gung Thang Plateau
And there became successful and wealthy.

Then an aunt and uncle arrived
And became dependent on us.
In childhood my father's death left us unsupported
And the aunt and uncle stole our food and wealth.

They worked my mother and us fatherless children like slaves,
Feeding us no better than you'd feed a dog,
And forcing us to spin wool from dawn until dusk.
Were I to tell the whole story,
Even my enemies would weep.

Due to these circumstances
I left the region of central Tibet
And completed the study of violent mantras,
The "Purple Basilisk,"[24] magical powers,
And the art of destruction by hailstorms
With Lama Yungtön Trogyal
And Doctor Nupchung of Rong.

I killed more than thirty people
In the circle of my aunt and uncle
And then devastated the countryside
By causing three feet of hail.

The instigator for all this was my mother.
Aside from mastering such evil mantras
I did not have the karmic fortune
To correctly study philosophy.
Such were my homes and early studies.

They pressed him further, "How did you encounter the dharma? Who is your lama? What is your lineage of practice? What empowerments and instructions did you receive?" Mila again replied in song:

> Lord of dharma who shines in my mind,
> Empower me with continual blessings.
>
> If your ears are not tired,
> Listen carefully, great scholars.
>
> Great Lama Yungton's
> Most devoted patron died.
> Because of this,
> He gave me provisions
> And sent me to Lama Rongton Lhaga
> To obtain the doctrine of the Great Perfection.[25]
>
> That wise and venerable person
> Revealed this prophesy to me:
> "Our karmic connection is finished.
> Your lama through beginningless births
> Has been the great teacher Lama Marpa."
>
> At the mere sound of his name my hair stood up;
> My mind for a while was stunned and numb.
> When, after much hardship, I finally met him,
> My whole outlook changed at first sight of his face.
> That great translator Marpa,
> Precious, peerless man of Lhodrak,
> Was indeed my lama in all my lives.
>
> My spiritual grandfather is great padit Naropa,
> And my spiritual great-grandfather is Tilo Sherab Sangbo.
> My mother is Vajrayogini,
> And my ultimate ancestor, Conqueror Vajradhara;
> Thus, my lineage is high, not low.

I stayed six years and eight months
With my lineaged lama Marpa.
As I had no wealth to give
I offered the constant services of mind and body.

By me alone, no longer youthful,
His son's house was constructed.
Six pillars, nine stories, a thirty-column courtyard,
I completed the whole structure
Except the minor details.

I was empowered and blessed successively
For father-tantra Guhyasamaja,
Nondual Hevajra tantra,
Heroic Buddha Kapala tantra,
And mother-tantra Mahamaya.

Also inner and outer Chakrasamvara,
The four Vajra positions, and so on,
Jetsun Vajrayogini,
Vajravarahi and the like,
Nairatmya and her twelve attendants,
And the twenty-one forms of goddess Tara.

In addition to these yoga-tantras
I received, unbroken and intact,
All empowerments and preliminary instructions
For kriya- and charya-tantras.

I also received the precepts
For the completion stage of peerless yoga-tantra,
And Naropa's path of method in particular—
The six essential yogas and so on—
The sequence of four developmental empowerments,
The completion stage of the liberative path of method,
The most secret stages of transference,

Removing obstructions, curing sickness, exercising pranas,
The Ear-whispered Tantras like the "Innate,"[26]
And the keys to mahamudra.

Again, the scholars asked, "Please tell us what kind of experience and realization you achieved through these empowerments and instructions for practice."
Mila replied:

Revealer of the essence of the natural state
Who set me on the path of reality,
Dharma lord of constant kindness,
To father buddha Marpa's feet I bow.

Great scholars with no mental guide,
I will reply to your search for facts;
Incline your ears and listen:

First, as instructed by my lama,
I meditated on this rare leisure and opportunity,
Understanding that it occurs once in a hundred births.
Then I meditated on impermanence and change
And understood whatever is impermanent will die.

I contemplated where I would be reborn after death
And knew that by the inevitable force of evil actions
I would be reborn in lower states
Where I would have no chance for freedom.

Because no protection from such fate exists
Other than the precious Triple Gem,
I took fervent refuge at the outset.
When I realized that there is no guide
Like my own precious lama,
I recalled his kindness and prayed to him.

Because I had no way to offer possessions
In worship to lama, deity, and Triple Gem,
I offered in imagination the mandala of Mt. Sumeru
And the four great continents,
With my own body freely given.

To cleanse my sins from beginningless time—
Evil powers, hailstorms, and the like—
I recited the hundred-syllable mantra
And made confession complete with the four strengths[27]
Until the signs of the purification of sins appeared.

Not stopping at mere intellectual knowledge
Of the gradual process of profound path teachings,
I practiced without regard for fatigue or strain
Until the signs and marks of progress appeared.
In one place, during a practice retreat,
I meditated strenuously for eleven months,
Never allowing my cushion to lose its warmth.

By the fruits of this cultivation,
The attachment which clings to a self was removed.
I realized that consciousness is essentially gnosis.
Mistaken patternings were purified into their original state,
And the natural state of gnosis was born within me.

I conceived compassion for those beings
Living amidst the press of illusion,
Blind to their true reality.
I conceived the supreme enlightenment-mind,
Itself no more than illusion,
Thinking: "Because they must be freed,
I will work for the welfare of these illusory beings."

I took this dreamlike, illusory body
To dwell in mountains barren of men,
And survived on nettles for many years,

Wrapped only in a robe of Nepalese cotton
While the bliss-warmth of tummo heat blazed
In my body which was free from all sickness.

Were I to tell you of my visions of the faces
Of personal deities, dreamlike and illusory,
Their voices resounding like echoes,
And the swirling clouds of warriors and dakinis,
It would be beyond numbering.
Yet all the while I remained in unwavering focus
On the natural state's unchanging reality.

The scholars asked again, "Please say something about the differences among the three commitments, the vow of personal liberation, the bodhisattva vow, and tantric vows."
To this, Mila replied:

Emanated bodies variously revealed,
Enjoyment-body spontaneously born,
Reality-body of preconception itself,
I bow to my lama who embodies all three.

To cut through the confusion behind your question,
Listen here, you two scholars
Who possess the roots of aspiration and faith:

First, because the seven classes
Of commitment to personal liberation
Only govern body and speech,
They last only as long as life itself;
After death the commitment is lost.

For novices and fully ordained monks,
If there occurs an unconfessed breach
Of any of the four main vows,[28]
The commitment to personal liberation is lost
And there is no way to regain it in this life.

But according to the bodhisattva viewpoint,
As long as afflictive emotions last,
Antidotes can be produced
With the intent to remove negativity.
Thus if any breach occurs
There are many ways to repair it.

The fruit of keeping this commitment
Ensures its occurrence again in the next rebirth,
While lapses yield corresponding results.

The bodhisattva commitment
Is conceived in the mind;
Thus, it lasts until liberation if unbroken.
If broken, it can be restored again.
Three times each day and night
Recite the *Sutra of the Three Aggregates*;[29]
Thus, in the eyes of bodhisattvas and conquerors,
The residue of one's lapses will be cleansed.

If major lapses have occurred,
Confess them in the visualized presence
Of Bodhisattva Akashagharba
And before someone who keeps the bodhisattva vows.
In the absence of a lama,
Renew the commitment before an image.

The fruit of keeping this commitment
Is spontaneous action for the vast welfare of beings
And attainment of perfect buddhahood
Through the lineage of bodhisattvas.
If broken, the bad results are very great.

At the onset of the process of Peerless Tantra
The lama carefully examines the student
And the student carefully examines the lama.
When a student who is qualified

And wants to learn
Asks a truly qualified lama three times
The series of four empowerments is conferred
To develop body, speech, and mind.

He tries to gain such entrance[30]
After performing various preparations
Aimed at repairing all breaches
In the bodhisattva commitment,
In the common and particular vows of the five meditation
　　bodhisattvas,
The Tantric Vehicle's fourteen major lapses,[31]
And in the major and minor breaches.

By the vase empowerment conferred on the body
One always stays directly involved
In identifying one's body with the deity's.

By the secret empowerment conferred on the voice
One hears all recited texts
As the deity's own void-sounding voice.

By the third empowerment of wisdom gnosis,
Well-conferred on the mind,
One is freed into the blissful state,
Of experiencing the natural progress of the four ecstasies.[32]

By conferring the fourth and supreme empowerment of words,
One becomes focused in the fabrication-free state
Through perception of the import of mahamudra.

If you keep intact the commitments and vows
After complete conferral of the four empowerments
You will receive the benefits of
All siddhis, both common and supreme.

As the supreme siddhi, one's own goal is attained,
The invincible state of spontaneous reality-body
Interpenetrating the whole of space.

And like a sun in space, the enjoyment-body
Is born, surrounded by its pure circle,
In densely packed Akanistha Heaven.
And from it the sunbeams
Of a multitude of emanated bodies
Stream to wherever unpurified trainees dwell.

Manifesting these three bodies
One becomes Vajradhara himself,
Endowed with five wisdoms and four bodies—
Those three bodies plus their essential unity.

In this life the bad results of breaking these commitments
Are disease and insanity,
Personal troubles, untimely death,
Leprosy, arthritis, and internal disorders.
Myriad miseries are bound to occur.

When your breath is about to stop,
Consciousness sinks and heads toward hell—
The one called Vajra Hell,
From which there is no chance of liberation.

When your own world meets destruction,
You will be reborn in worlds to the east,
Then south, west, and north,
In between, below, and above.

If you cannot stand the pain of a mere thorn,
How will you endure the spinning saws?

If you cannot stand the pain of a mere spark,
How will you endure the ground of blazing iron?

If you cannot stand your soup too hot,
How will you endure the drink of molten copper?

If it can not be borne, it must be avoided;
Thus, of all three types of commitment,
That of the empowerments is most critical by far.
If you understand well the keys
To practice without disturbing your vows,
Then in this life, at death, in the intermediate state,
Or in seven or sixteen more lifetimes at most,
Liberation will be attained
And the powers of Vajradhara gained.

But if this is not achieved,
Faults may occur that damage your vows
And you are quickly set back a long way.

Because the source of all achievement
Is none other than your holy lama,
You should view your lama as Buddha himself
And always strive to please
With service and every possible thing;
Never dare to cause displeasure.

If you transgress your vows
With anger, aggression, or criticism
Toward your vajra-brothers and sisters,[33] close and far,
Who entered the mandala with you
Or those who entered before and after,
This will cause a fall to the lowest hell.

Although transgression of vows,
Both major and minor,
May be repaired through intense regret,
Strive to keep them intact.

If you want to know in breadth and detail
The process of practice and the keys

To all these things,
Serve a lama who's truly qualified,
Compassionate, and skilled in method.

I have just explained the tip of this.
If I explained it fully, where would it end?

The scholars then said, "Of the three commitments, the commitment to personal liberation of the Lesser Vehicle is limited to one's own liberation and does not provide the great waves of benefit for others. The bodhisattva's commitment of the Great Vehicle takes many, many eons. The unsurpassed vehicle of Peerless Tantra is fast, but extremely dangerous. Would you explain the real reason for this?" They bowed and offered a mandala, and this song arose in the precious lama's throat:

I bow to kind Marpa's three spontaneous bodies:
The inherent reality-body arrived at the true homeland,
The enjoyment-body in the fastness of Akanistha Heaven,
And emanated bodies mercifully streaming to the ten
    directions.

If you do not know how to open meaning's iron door
With the key of consummate verbal skill
In the basic points of Buddha's teachings,
Incline your ears and listen well.

To soar in mahamudra's vast sky,
Nourish body with the food of vase empowerment
And slake thirst with the nectar of secret empowerment.
Then, after raising the bliss-void mind of wisdom
    empowerment
And spreading the method-wisdom wings of word
    empowerment,
Fly into the sky of the natural state.

If you want to enter the mansion
Of this natural state, how can you do it
Without opening the door of empowerment?

Mahamudra can be cultivated
In two ways:
The gradual and the sudden.

To follow the gradual way
Begin with refuge and mind-for-enlightenment
And progress by stages
Through preparatory, realizational, and post-attainment states.

After opening empowerment's door,
Perfect the states of concentration and practice
As pointed out, stage by stage,
By a lama possessed of such experience.

For persons having the good fortune
Of merit acquired in previous lives
The four empowerments may be conferred at once
And the sudden way pointed out.

In either case, until the goal is reached,
The extent of training and study,
The varying dispositions of practitioners,
Differences in action, dedication, and karmic connection,
Even food and daily behavior,
Will determine progress, the way meditation is achieved,
Its duration, decrease, and cessation,
Thought-flow, excitement, depression,
And the varieties of hindrance and obstruction—
You need a lama who is experienced
In dealing with all these things.

The voidness experienced in the natural state
Is void in a number of different ways,
None of which leave the domain of voidness.
The sixteen types of voidness
Can be condensed into four, or three:
The flash of voidness through force of intellect,

The voidness of the cessation of associative cognition,
And ultimate, complete voidness.

Much could be said about all this,
But this is not the time to do it.
In brief, the mahamudra
Is essentially the same
As the precious fourth empowerment of words.
Without empowerment, how can it be done?

Without initiation and empowerment, holy Dharma,
However deep, will not lead to a meaningful goal.
Like a man without a head,
Practice without empowerment leads to lower states.
And I have already explained what happens if you
Break your vows after empowerment.

With great faith they begged him, "We want to rely on you, precious
Jetsun lama. Be our guide to this quick path in both this life and the next."

The scholars left and, on the twenty-seventh day of the following month,
returned with pack animals and porters. In front of Jetsun and his disciples
the two scholars prepared an elaborate circle feast and chanted this request:

In Tibet, abundant land of snows,
In the province of Tsang,
The district of Selmo,
On the slopes of Red Rock, heap of jewels,
On the great mountain Trashi Ghentsen
Stands the wondrous rock called Horse's Hoof.
In it, in this delightful self-born cave,
Sits a most marvelous and holy man.

Oh repa, are you not an emanation?
Unaffected by physical affliction,
Living with no food at all,
Naked body suffused with brilliance—
We bow in praise to your vajra-body.

We bow to the dharma rainfall of your speech,
The pure beauty of your void-sounding voice
Spreading the petals of your lotus throat
And opening your treasury of vajra-song.

We bow to your unconditional wisdom and mercy,
Your awareness focused in reality,
But wasting no time when teaching beings
From your dharma-realm state of gnosis.

Your mind penetrates everything knowable
With the essence of great compassion.
Remember us with mercy
From your state of changeless reality.

Driven by actions and afflictive emotions,
We have been adrift since beginningless time
On the vast ocean of samsara,
Tasting the many pains of illusory life.

Oblivious to the selfless natural state,
We have taken the illusory and false as real,
And, possessed by the demon of afflictive emotions,
We cut the throat of our own blissful liberation.

We traveled the perilous path of transitional states,
Plunged into the abyss of the three lower realms,
And sank into the mire of the ten sinful actions
Redolent with miseries difficult to bear.

Now, through the saving grace
Of a little moral practice in previous lives
We have the leisure and opportunity of human life.

This leisure and opportunity obtained by chance,
Was spent during youth on children's folly.
Then, grown older, we became scholars

And learned the ways of logical argument
Which involved us in the eight worldly concerns.

We clarified the teachings
With the cleansing of well-reasoned dharma,
But were perched on the lofty peak of self-esteem
With pride in our infinitesimal knowledge.

When defeated in debate by a skillful opponent,
We were unhappy and dejected.
When others were considered better than us,
We were plunged into the briarpatch of envy.

Although skillful in the use of words
We had not been face to face with the natural state.
Lacking this experience of the actual state
We were mere winnowers of empty chalf.

Now, in this boat of human leisure and chance,
Please prepare for us the conditions
For our escape from the ocean of samsara.
We will rely on you, precious guide
And saviour of beings.

Guide us with great compassion!
Look after us with the eye of wisdom!
Quickly take us in hand!

They were moved to tears with powerful emotion. The great Jetsun, with
blazing body and powerful voice, sang this song from the unchanging state
of clear light:

I bow to my Dharma lord and lama,
In the fabricated mansion of the dharma-realm,
Whose spontaneous body of unchanging great bliss
Emits emanations for compassionate works.

As the lotus of your awareness,
Grown from the strong roots of faith
And nurtured by the moist warmth of aspiration,
Opens its buds in the light of intellect,
In the abundant sweetness of its scent
The darting bees of my mind
Sound the melodious buzzing
Of this song of renunciation.

If you really intend to practice,
Your homeland is the devil's prison—
Cast it all behind you.

Food and possessions are ties to samsara;
Cut them off with the sword of nonattachment.

Relations are an obstructive spell;
Keep determination foremost in mind.

Lovers are the devil's envoys;
Turn away with strong resolution.

Distraction is a practitioner's stepmother;
Isolate yourself with strong determination.

While meditating mahamudra,
Abandon physical and verbal activities.

If you want experience and realization,
You must bear hardship, suffering, and fear.

If you listen to what I have said,
You two will have fortunate karma.
I will confer initiatory empowerments and blessings,
Impart the precepts of the profound ear-whispered tantras,
And bestow the essence of profound precepts.
Teacher and students will merge in practice and view.

Through the action and supplication prepared in this life,
And the karma and supplication extending
Into the pure realm of the next,
May you experience the truth of reality
And act spontaneously for the sake of all beings.

Thus, two scholars upholding the doctrine,
Remember these things I have told you;
Apply them well in practice.

In extreme joy they said, "Great Jetsun, although we may not be able to practice like that, we will try to follow your words. Please give us the key instructions for the profound path, along with the initiatory empowerments."

So Mila gave them step-by-step empowerments and instructions for practicing the profound path. They renounced worldly affairs and practiced one-pointedly until the signs and assets of progress appeared. Both eventually became excellent yogins.

Mila's Meeting with Drigom Repa

One day, as the great yogin Lord Milarepa was practicing in Lower Hollow Cave of Lachi, the yogin Drigom Repa arrived. Jetsun asked him, "Where are you from?"

He replied, "I have come from the region of Dri Khung."

"What are you doing here?"

"I heard that a siddha named Lord Milarepa was living in the area. He does not know much about philosophy and the like, but I intend to ask him for meditation instruction. Where is he staying now?"

Jetsun replied, "I am Milarepa."

"Very good." Drigom Repa seemed unimpressed by this news, but he paid his respects and knelt for a blessing. He then said, "Great siddha-yogin, through your experience of mahamudra you have untangled channels of your throat center and acquired great renown as a treasury of vajra-song. Consider singing me a song to establish our dharma relationship."

So Mila sang:

> Precious Jetsun with the eye of wisdom,
> Dharma Lord Marpa, ever-kind teacher,
> I fervently pray, grant me the blessings of my lineage
> And free all beings from the ocean of misery.
>
> Listen a bit, Drigom, without distraction:
> In this age when the five degeneracies prevail,[34]
> Can our impulsive, perverse behavior
> Provide an opportunity to gain stability of mind?

Our unwholesome habit of feeling
Attraction and aversion is caused by life's desires
Imprinted on our minds from beginningless time—
Will this help us to be virtuous and abandon evil?

A worldly lama interested only in gain,
Having heard a month's teachings and practiced one year,
Mouths empty words—
Is this an "expert meditator" experienced in tranquilization?

Lacking the calm ocean of lucid tranquilization,
The ornaments of bliss, clarity, and freedom from thought,
And the solidness of an immobile mountain—
Do you mistake mental blankness for meditation?

Unskilled in the keys to explicit and implicit meanings[35]
Because you lack wisdom that probes the natural state's
    essence,
Do you mistake tranquility's natural lucidity, brilliance and
    clarity
For actual insight and integration?[36]

For a "lama" of skill and achievement
Who has realized such tranquilization and insight,
But still lacks experience and skill in teaching,
How could the title "lama" even apply?

Lacking genuine admiration and respect
For lamas who have tasted the experience of purity,
Do you fail to view them as buddhas,
And believe instead that they are ordinary lamas?

Failing to understand that *all* the actions of such lamas,
Both good and bad, are virtuous,
Do you ever think they are wrong, even for an instant,
And despise them in the slightest?

Not holding one's lama dearer than life,
Not realizing the abuse they receive is their own fault,
Such disciples are critical of the smallest thing.
Aren't they numerous these days?

They put off realization and experience to future lives,
In this life they encounter much misery;
Such disciples are asking for the hell of unceasing torment.

Thus you must seek a lama
Greater than me in power and skill.
Give up your worldly ideas and exert yourself in meditation.
May you have the fortune of health and culmination of
    practice.

Upon hearing this song, Drigom Repa was inspired with strong faith and said, "Precious lama, I came here intending to meet you. Whether you are praised or criticized, you are still a wise lama."

Thereupon Jetsun gave him initiation, taught him dharma, and gave him step-by-step instructions for meditation. He later became an accomplished siddha.

Song of the Peacock

In the Buddhist tradition the peacock symbolizes the bodhisattva's practice of "utilizing poisons on the path." This is the basic principle of tantric practice. It involves the deliberate use of negative emotions and conditions to accelerate mental development, like the peacock, who is said to eat poisonous plants to improve its plumage. Such practice is difficult and dangerous; the protection inherent in the mind truly aimed at enlightenment is necessary before this should be attempted. Mila's gesture of neutralizing the priest's afflictions by "consuming" his poisons is an extension of this peacock-bodhisattva analogy. This story also appears in a slightly different version in Mila's autobiography.

Milarepa was generally disliked by all the Bön priests of Nya Nang and Drin. One of these evil-minded priests mixed a poison powder into a bowlful of yoghurt and gave it to a leper woman, telling her, "Offer this to Jetsun." The priest paid her a turquoise gem in return for this favor.

When she offered the yoghurt, Jetsun said, "I will drink this so that you may earn the turquoise. Because you did not know it was poisoned, you will not suffer any harmful consequences." He washed the bowl out and gave it back saying, "I cannot offer the remainder to you."[37]

"Why is that?" asked Shengom Repa. Mila replied with this song:

> I bow to my royal doctor, my lama
> Who revealed his three supreme dimensions
> By curing the sick torment of the three poisons
> With the medicine of the three vehicles.

Like the peacock,
I spread the wings of method and wisdom
From a state of natural realization.
A crest of radiant self-illumination
Adorns the head of supreme gnosis
Which rests on the long neck of the ever-present void.

My golden beak shines with good qualities,
My two bright eyes see both realities.[38]
A variety of colors in my long tail feathers
Symbolizes the five gnoses, which
Provide benefit to all,
And my two feet are the knowledge
Of what to accept and what to reject.

Consuming the virulent poison in an offering
Tainted by the three afflictive poisons,
This peacock of the actual state
Relieves the afflictions of the donor.
May he be freed from the darkness of the three poisons.

Tell that Bön priest
"Though you may not like it,
I will be staying on this earth a while longer."

In tears, the leper woman beat her breast. Jetsun told her, "You had no bad intention, so you will incur no consequence at all. Do not cry." At that he became slightly sick, but was cured through the care of his disciples.

Fourfold Song of Precepts

Traveling upward through Chupak on Pelmo Plateau with young Seben Repa, the great Jetsun went to beg at a large encampment. They told him, "Sing us a song, then we will give you food." So Mila sang this song:

Homage and praise to my father lamas.

You fortunate patrons seated here
Have asked me to sing a song.
I now offer a fourfold song of precepts.

Some of you patrons seated here
Have asked, "Where are you from? Where are you going?
Where do you stay? What do you do? Who are your friends?
What possessions do you have? Tell us."

Others have asked me,
"Fashion some dharma into song
To urge us on to holy dharma."
Whatever the question, listen now:

I arrived this morning from Lachi mountain.
I have no plan to go anywhere else.
I live on mountains, promoting good practice.
My work is to help beings impartially.

I have twenty-one good friends:
Buddha, dharma, and holy community,
Embodied by my compassionate lama,
Are my three friends granting refuge.

Deities Samvara, Hevajra, and Guhyasamaja
Are my three friends on the production stage;
And currents, channels, and drops are
My three friends revealing the path of method.[39]

View, meditation, and practice
Are my three friends for engaging in action;
And warriors, dakinis, and protectors are
My three friends for removing obstructions.

Discipline, illuminating science, and transcendences[40]
Are my three friends in learning;
And dedication, supplication, and good wishes are
My three friends that nourish virtue's root.

I wander the countryside aimlessly;
I have left homeland without regrets.
Having consorted with "mother"[41] and dakinis,
I have left mother and sister without regrets.
Having relied on flint and iron striker,
I've left hearth-fire without regrets.
Having donned this square cotton robe,
I've left fine brocades with no regrets.

Having eaten a lot of wild leeks,
I've left meat, butter and grain with no regret.
After drinking at cool mountain streams,
I've left tea and beer with no regret.
After seeing changeless reality,
I've left worldly affairs with no regret.

That was my first song of precepts,
My story of yogic awareness

In reply to your questions.
Now I'll sing about human affairs:[42]

The best men among you, if lacking religion,
Are like vultures flying in the sky—
Lofty thoughts, but insignificant.

Average men, if lacking dharma,
Are like the striped tigers of India—
Great strength, but insignificant.

Inferior men, if lacking dharma,
Are like grey wolves of the north—
Great hardiness, but insignificant.

The best of women, if lacking dharma,
Are like brown mice nesting in walls—
Skilled in acquisition, but insignificant.

Average women, if lacking dharma,
Are like sneaky graveyard foxes—
Much activity, but insignificant.

Inferior women, if lacking dharma,
Are like paintings on a wall—
Fine in form, but insignificant.

A person who ignores religion, though born a human,
Is an old bull eating human food.

Virile men lacking dharma
Are oxen decorated with armor.

Women lacking dharma
Are cows decorated with ribbons.

Young girls lacking dharma
Are heifers wearing ornaments.

Children lacking dharma
Are calves with bristling neck hair.

That is my second song of precepts;
Now I will sing some poetic metaphors:

In the three summer months the sun king blazes.
When the sky becomes cloaked in cloud,
The thunder dragon rumbles,
And rain falls soft and gentle.
Why should the royal blue peacocks
Not bend back their necks?

In winter the earth loses its life-breath.
When, in the new year, pierced by cold winds,
The sky becomes clear and free from clouds,
And seven horses draw up the shining sun,
Flooding the earth with warm rays,
Why should the poorly clothed
Who suffer cold not rejoice?

In autumn months the king of time shines.
Fruit and grain grow ripe;
Mountains are not yet clothed in snow.
In a pleasant, quiet place,
Free from hardship and danger,
Why shouldn't birds and deer
Be happy and playful?

In spring the sun moves north.
When granaries are empty
And famine strikes,
If food and drink are given
To those hungry and starving,
Why would they not be happy?

After circling samsara again and again,
Birth and death alternating

Like the seasonal miseries of heat and cold,
When you are given some helpful advice
To convince you of impermanence,
Why not be joyful?

That is my song of poetic metaphors,
My third song of precepts.
Now I will sing a song of warning:

In summer when pigs and foxes flee together,
Floods are coming, oh householders.

In autumn when the hay barn is dry,
Fire might strike, oh farmers.

In the new year when cold winds blow,
Wind storms are coming, oh tent dwellers.

When the life force is exhausted,
Death will soon arrive, oh gods and men.

That is my song of precepts;
My fourth song of precepts.

Let my precepts of friendly persuasion
Be a teaching of death for the aged,
An enjoyable song for men,
An injunction to virtue for women,
A love song for virile youths,
A pretty song for young girls,
And a nursery rhyme for children.
If you have the fortune, let it urge you to virtue.

All patrons, men and women seated here,
I pray for your fortune and harmony with dharma.

Everyone was filled with strong faith. Mila stayed there for several days, helping those people by means of his spiritual connection with them.

Mila Tests the Determination of Two Women

Mila's treatment of women often seemed unnecessarily harsh and sexist. In this story he responds to the two women with painfully direct criticisms of a woman's role in Tibetan society. His rough treatment was actually a test of their ability to recognize their cultural conditioning and their willingness to end it. This was often true in his treatment of men as well as women, and once a woman understood the extent of his criticism—which was actually social, not sexual—she could become a fully qualified disciple. A number of such women became accomplished yoginis under his guidance.

Once Jetsun Milarepa, great lord of yogins, was staying at White Rock Horse Tooth cave with his "son" and disciple, Rechungpa. One sunny day a woman arrived with a young girl. After greeting him, they bowed many times.

"I have taken you for my refuge from samsara," the woman said. "Though husband and sons were very angry, I have come to you, great Jetsun, to ask for dharma. This girl is my neighbor and she has also come to ask for dharma." Saying this, she offered a valuable turquoise.

Jetsun responded with the usual scriptural recitation and said, "Samsara is basically miserable, and women are particularly exposed to it. Quarreling and fighting are your reality especially when you have a family. What are your names?"

The woman replied, "My name is Reality Woman, and she is Wisdom Girl."

Jetsun sat a moment, thinking with eyes closed, and then said, "Dharma is difficult for those predisposed to it. For women it is usually even more difficult. I will tell you the reasons for this in a song. Pay attention! Listen." And Mila sang:

I bow to the feet of Marpa, best of men,
Emanation-body of great Vajradhara.

In the empty house of your illusory body
Your mind has been afflicted with illusions of ego.
Because of egoism you desire children
And take on a mate in marriage.

You drink deep the draught of desire,
Strike with the vicious weapon of hatred,
Tie the black silk of delusion round your head,
And sit upon the throne of pride.

You eat the afflictive food of jealousy,
Hoard the wealth of the ten evils,[43]
Make your way home to the three low states,
And experience intense misery.

Throughout the four seasons you farm
With the twelve links of dependent occurrence.
From the seeds of habituation
You raise crops of illusion and wrong thinking
And ripen the fruits of preconception and affliction.

Within the hollow of your sex
Flows the blood of elemental desire.
Blown by the winds of such conditioning
You're always looking over your shoulder,
Frown becomes smile like summer weather,
Mouth constantly flutters like a bird in springtime;
Your body gestures like an actor.

But acting out these desires
Only brings misery;

You labor like a slave for your own satisfaction,
Caught in the poisonous whirlpool of desire.

A bardo voyager, your unborn child
Has sapped the shine and vigor of your body.
For nine months you hold it in your womb
And during birth experience intense pain.

Then you have the troubles of upbringing.
Powerless to remove this burden from your back,
Unable to still their harsh retorts,
Unable to live without working for them,
What would you do without your "dear" children?

Your mind is overcome
With unnecessary necessities;
You anxiously weigh each bushel of barley
And see loss and gain in a handful of grain.

Acting with deceit and pretension,
Mouthing slander, nonsense, and lies,
The three evil poisons mixing in mind,
You are like the family dog.

You do not even know what is evil.
Evil is like a bird flying in the sky;
When taking to the sky,
Its shadow follows on the ground,
And when the bird lights on a tree
Its shadow arrives right below.

Hoarded food and wealth are carried off by others.
But the burden of evils must be borne by yourself.
There is no situation worse than this.

This is why practice would be hard for you;
Therefore, it is best to return to your homes.

But they did not heed this advice, and through Mila's instruction, they achieved excellent realization, eventually becoming expert meditators concerned solely with practice.

The Ups and Downs of Samsara

Once in early summer the great Jetsun descended into the region of upper Tingri to beg. Entering the square of a village, he encountered a group of people and asked, "Have you any food?"

They replied, "Sing us a penetrating song and we will give you food."

So Jetsun sang them this song:

> I humbly pray to you,
> Holy lama who knows past, present, and future,
> Lord of love and compassion,
> Guide me with unwavering attention.
>
> All you fortunate ones gathered here—
> Listen with undistracted attention:
>
> When the command of the new year's king descends,
> The focused brilliance of moon-ministers fades,
> And the massed armies of passing days' inexorable advance
> Slash the life force's flowing breath
> With the sharp weapons of each fleeting moment,
> Know that the first warning has been given!
>
> Led by faulty vision of this life's affairs,
> You're confused about what is and is not to be done.
> Unable to distinguish virtue from evil,
> You continually seek sustenance by wrong means.

When the flow of your breath stops
There is danger of rebirth in animal realms.
Know that the second warning has been given!

Bound by the shackle of attachment to life
You're unable to give even one mere sesame seed.
Unscrupulously seeking others' possessions,
You sustain yourselves with lies and deceit.
When the formative forces of this brief life run out
You are certain to take rebirth among frustrated spirits.
Know that the third warning has been given!

Drunk with the poisonous waters of strong hatred,
You take others' lives for food and wealth
And sustain your own life with evil food.
When it's time to leave for the next world,
You are sure to taste the torments of hell.
Know that the fourth warning has been given!

On hearing this song of four warnings, many young female patrons paid respects. With tears running down their faces they said, "Precious lama, our behavior has not been in accord with the lama's teachings. It is a great fault and very wrong. Please tell what miseries will befall us if we are born in lower states."

Mila replied with this song:

I pray with fervent admiration
To my supreme lama and triple gem.

If you have done small, vicious actions
Motivated by basic delusion,
You will be reborn in the low state of animals.

Eating each other,
And the unimaginable anxiety of having no refuge
Are the main miseries which must be faced there.
You react to everything as if it were an enemy.

Helpless, you will be killed by others,
Usually for your flesh and skin,
Sometimes for your pearly bones,
And sometimes for your fleece and hair.

At times captive under the hand of man,
Nose pierced, burdened, ridden, hitched to ploughs,
Driven by whip and goad—
The details of such sufferings are unthinkable.

Prevalent miseries of extreme temperature change,
Summer, winter, autumn, spring;
Cold at night, hot in the day,
And intermittent pains of birth and death
Felt many times each day.

Life among animals is like dried malt
Tumbling in a beer bottle on the ocean—
Its miseries are beyond imagination.

If you have done moderately vicious acts
Motivated by desire and greed
You will wander low states of frustrated spirits.

Tormenting karmic retribution must be faced:
In winter the sun is cold,
In summer the moon burns like fire,
Rivers run dry at a glance,
And forests appear as charred rubble.
Rain falls on your body like hot sand,
Lightning and hail fall like rain.

Body wasted and weakened by hunger,
Ugly hair shaggy as a horse's mane,
Your two deep, sunken eyes stare out,
Like stars, from deep within their sockets.

Some frustrated spirits have mountain-sized stomachs
And throats as thin as the string of a bow.
Stumbling on, wasted by hunger,
Unable to find even scraps of garbage,
Their hunger pangs are unthinkable.

At night, for some, fire burns in the mouth,
Skin shrinks to the bone, and, when moving,
Embers smolder in the eight great joints.
They run in thirst to the edge of a stream
Of trickling water, but it stops
And they are pelted by a cyclone of intensely hot sand.

Others have goiters the size of Mount Everest
On bodies as tiny as atoms;
For food they try to suck the blood and pus
Oozing from their own goiters.
The torments of spirits like these
Are far beyond the imagination.

If you have committed many vicious acts
Motivated by intense hatred,
You will face the miseries of hell beings.

There are hot hells, cold hells,
Day hells, and intermediate hells—four types in all.

There are eight hot hells:
Those of Repeated Revival, Black Lines,
Crushing, Wailing, Loud Wailing,
Hot, Intensely Hot, and Ceaseless Torment.

All beings become enemies on sight.
Whatever they pick up becomes a weapon
And, striking each other, all are felled.
Then the sky resounds with a reviving thunder

And they arise again and behave as before.
The hell where this is faced a thousand-million times
Each day is called Repeated Revival.

Black lines divide the body eight ways
And are cut through with burning saws;
Such sufferers are beings of the Black Line Hell.

Having been battered against an iron mountain
By six goat- and sheep-headed hellguards,
Twisted and squashed like a bug,
One's body revives and such torment continues;
This hell is called Crushing Hell.

In the Hell of Wailing you will face the agony
Of being impaled through your forehead
With burning iron stakes.
In the Hell of Loud Wailing you are agonized
By being impaled through your head and both shoulders
With the prongs of blazing tridents.

In the Hot Hell you'll face continual pains
Such as burning inside a doorless, iron house
Where you will jump violently about,
Mouth and nose choking with smoke,
Bones of feet crackling to pieces,
Body oozing blood and fat.

In the hell called Intensely Hot,
In a two-storied house of flaming iron,
The mouths of some, opened by glowing clamps,
Are filled down to their guts
With fiercely boiling molten copper.
Others are fried

In blazing pots of iron.

Swirling red and black masses of flame
Like the fiery winds which consume worlds at time's end
Rush in from all quarters
With an intense and fearful roar.
Except for this harsh, piercing sound,
All is consumed in a mass of flame.
There is no agony worse than this
Continual burning without relief.
Thus, this hell is called Ceaseless Torment.

All hot hells have in common the miseries
Of being afflicted by mankind's diseases,
Loud, terrifying sounds,
And grounds of burning iron.

Outside these hell worlds
And everywhere between
Lie the intermediate hells:
Glowing Embers, Rotten Corpse Swamp,
Knife Trees, and Uncrossable River.
And scattered everywhere lie the day hells
Which are endured for only one day.

The eight cold hells are: The Blistering,
Bursting Blisters, Achu, Kyihu,
Cracking Teeth, Splitting Like a Poppy,
Splitting Like a Lotus, and Splitting Like a Peony.

Weakened by the cold of icy currents and snows
At the miserable depths of oceans
And at the earth's poles,
Blisters break out.
As it grows colder they burst.

When the cold gets more intense only "achu" is heard.
Exhausted by cold, only "kyihu" is heard.
With extreme freezing teeth crack.

In near-absolute cold the body splits
Into four pieces like a poppy,
Then further into six and eight like a lotus.
Finally it splits into 100,000 like a peony
In the intensity of absolute cold.

I have thus illustrated just a drop
From the vast ocean of misery
Of the three lower realms.

Now consider while you still have the chance:
If you can not bear even one glowing spark,
Could you stand the ground of blazing iron?

If you can not bear even one thorn,
Could you stand the flaming iron stakes?

If you can not bear even one hot drop,
Could you stand the violently boiling water?

If you can not bear the scorching sun's heat,
Could you stand the torments of the hot hells?

If you can not bear the winter's freezing wind,
Could you stand the pain of the cold hells?

If you can not bear your belly's occasional hunger,
Could you stand the continual torments of the pretas?

If you can not bear even minor fatigue,
Could you stand the sufferings of animals?

If you think these retributions are untrue
Consider the pleasures and sorrows of human life.
Know that the in- and out-flow of breath alone
Divides this life from the next.

Results of good and bad actions pursue us
Like a bird's shadow on the ground.
Results of virtues and vices are separately experienced
Like sweet and sour fruit propagated by their own seeds.

Consider now what you have done!
Ask yourselves, "Where will I go?"
Milarepa who wanders the countryside
Has sung his yogi's song to answer
Your question about the miseries of low states,
All you men and women patrons here,
And especially you young women of faith.

May this be the dharma-share of the faithfully devoted.
May this urge you to the religion of the thoughtful.
May this be a wisdom-text for smart men and women.
I pray for your fortune and success in dharma.

Again the women patrons paid respect and asked him, "Precious lama,
please continue and tell us a bit about the advantages of higher states." So
Jetsun sang them another song:

Listen further, faithful ones.
Bear this in mind, curious ones.

When you practice the six transcendences
While refraining from the ten vices,
Giving yields enjoyable possessions
And morality yields higher states of life.

By patience a good body is obtained,
Vigor is the source of swiftness.
Absorption pacifies the mind,
And through wisdom the natural state is realized.

Giving, morality, and patience
Are sources of merit;
Absorption and wisdom
Are sources of great gnosis;
And vigor furthers them all.

To the extent you accumulate meritorious action
You will be reborn in the three higher states.
And from there, if unwavering absorption
Is cultivated, you will be reborn
On levels in the form and formless realms
According to your past action.

There are four classes of humans,
Six levels of gods in the desire realm,
Seventeen levels in the form realm,
And four in the formless realm.

This is not the time to elaborate
About their types, lifespan,
Bodies, environments, and so on.

Complete buddhahood is attained
After traveling the five paths and ten stages
Through practice of the first five transcendences,
All focused by pure wisdom.

Concerning this, faithful ladies,
Practice these exhortations for virtue:

Give many gifts, impartially,
And without thought of return.

Maintain faultless morality
And keep the vows of purification[44]
On the full moon, new moon, and eight days thereafter.

Press on in the direction of virtue
By cultivating patience with strong vigor.

Following a lama of experience,
Meditate on the absorptions.
Slash presumptions about reality
With profound wisdom realizing the natural state.

Sustain unshakable faith,
The root of all this;
As the source of all attainment
Is the holy lama, visualize him
On the crown of your head, unmoving.

Make fervent confession and firm resolve
Concerning all obstructive faults and evils.
Rejoice in all virtue and merit
Acquired by others.

And stamp the seal of identitylessness
On all root-virtues, great or small,
With pure dedication and supplication.

Take these helpful precepts
Firmly into your hands.

The women were inspired with strong faith and placed Mila's feet on their heads. They rendered him excellent service and respect. For one month they sought initiations and instruction from him, catching a glimpse of the natural state of mind and gaining a foothold on the path.

Then, when Jetsun was about to leave, they caught hold of his feet and wept. He sang to them:

Listen here, faithful women:

In general, all things composed must disperse.
In particular, one's circle of friends must scatter.
Look again and again into mind's changeless essence!
When conceptual patterns are pure as space,
That is real *seeing*.

In general, all things acquired are lost.
In particular, our lives dwindle moment by moment.
Open the door to the inexhaustible treasury of gnosis!
When awareness and openness are inseparably united,
That is freedom from loss.

In general, all things born must die.
In particular, this resultant illusory body will surely die.
Seek and find the indestructible vajra-body!
When the three bodies are spontaneously achieved,
That is freedom from death.

May your minds attain this, faithful ladies.
We were brought together through action in prior lives;
Now, through the resolve to meet again,
I pray we be joined in the pure realm in later lives.

I offer this song of worship, holy lama!
Share in this feast of sound, host of dakinis!
Remove your obstructions, nonhumans!
Attend this auspicious song of worship!

Mila then left for the isolated mountain ranges.

PART THREE

SONGS OF REALIZATION

Experiences in Practice

In addition to communicating the essence of his own realization, a teacher must be able to judge the depth of his students' experience. The pieces in this section deal with problems and questions of Mila's advanced students. "Mila's Approval of Rechungpa" is an unusual glimpse into the relationship of Mila and his closest disciple. Independent and willful in nature, Rechungpa frequently bore the brunt of Mila's scathing criticism, as in "Rechungpa's Pride" (see Part Two). The present story is unique in its depiction of Mila's delight in Rechungpa's accomplishment. This unprecedented praise acknowledged Rechungpa's ability to take action in the realm of apparent phenomena without losing his focus on the natural state wherein perception is unstructured by such conditioned fabrications. This was an indication of his advancement from the production phase to the completion phase of tantric meditation.

Tantric practice is divided into these two phases, termed *production* and *completion*. The production phase is undertaken after the practitioner has attained stable concentration (shi.gnas) and compassion (nying.rje), and involves visualization of tantric deities (yidam) and their environments, followed by identification of the practitioner's mind with the mental reality of the deity (termed *divine pride*). This is practiced in conjunction with subsidiary techniques such as the Six Yogas of Naropa. The basic principle of identification of the practitioner's body and mind with the deity's is expressed in "Mila Reveals His Attainment":

> The various human foods,
> After conversion to pure nectar,
> Become continual nectar offerings
> To the divine mandala of the body.

The experiences of the production phase, though powerful and impressive, still fall within the realm of superficial phenomena; they are merely the results of tampering with the mechanisms of conditioned perception. In "Milarepa in Lhasa," he explains the sequence of development, from manipulating our perception of the phenomenal world to the penetration of the phenomenal, the "triumph over appearances."

Mila tells us, ". . . about reality itself nothing can be said," but he did talk about its relation to the apparent world:

Reality, when really viewed,
When really seen, is liberation.

This is a fundamental principle of the completion phase: the superficial world, when correctly seen, is a source of insight leading to ultimate realization. The yogin advances by repeated experience of the apparent world unstructured by conditioned patternings. The ultimate and the ordinary interpenetrate; they are defined by our perception. The conditioned mind's patterning of perception "creates" the apparent world, but in an ultimate sense nothing is created. In "Appearances and Mind," a student asks Mila, "Are all these appearances merely mental?" Mila replies that in the clarity of the natural state, the distinction between "merely mental" and "substantial" is irrelevant, because the mind's compulsion for dualistic patterning of experience has been defused. But because it is a grave error to underestimate the power of the conditionings, Mila continues with a series of precepts about the necessity of relating appropriately to the superficial world until the experience of the natural state has been firmly grasped. Freedom from conditionings cannot be won by ignoring them. But gradually, by alternating experience of the apparent world and its ultimate voidness, the mundane and the transcendent become integrated. The patterning of perception is no longer automatic and compulsive:

Attached to illusion they are "beings;"
Freed from illusion they are "buddhas."

This final integration is symbolized by the mandala, in which the superficial and transcendent aspects of reality are united as an offering, a sacrifice, born from effort and attitude, from one realm to the other.

120

Mila's Approval of Rechungpa

The great Jetsun lama and his disciple-son, Rechungpa Dorje Dragpa, were living at the Belly Cave of Nya Nang. One day, Rechungpa was sitting alone in meditation outside the door of the cave; Milarepa was inside. The lama called to him, "Rechungpa, come quickly!"

He came and saw that the cave's keystone was slipping. Milarepa, supporting it with both hands, cried out, "Quickly, put up a pillar!"

Rechungpa, still absorbed in primal voidness, hefted a boulder as big as a yak from the doorway of the cave and set it up as a pillar. The lama removed his hands, leaving their impression in the rock. This exists even to this day, and the great boulder is known as "Strong Man Rechungpa's Rock."

The lama then leaned to one side and supporting his body with his left hand, placed his right on Rechungpa's head. He sang this song:

> Dharma master who satisfies by mere memory,
> Translator who satisfies on mere hearing,
> Thanks for your kindness, Teacher Marpa!
> Grant me blessings, Compassionate One!
>
> Listen, Lama Rechungpa!
> Listen, Lama Dorje Dragpa!
> There are many called "lama,"
> But none like teacher Marpa,
> Embodiment of great Vajradhara.

There are many called "yogin,"
But none like Milarepa,
Who took up practices given by his lama
And faced the challenge heedless of body or life.

Surviving on mountain nettles
In unpopulated practice sites,
I have sometimes slept on thorns in snow mountains,
Warm bliss of tummo aflame in my body,
Voice proclaiming self-sound of vajra,
Mind absorbed in the natural state.
I have no fear at all of obstruction by demons.

Many are called "repa,"
But none like Dorje Dragpa,
Beautiful skin, face like a god's son,
Intellect brilliant like the sun and the moon,
And unyielding courage like Mount Everest itself,
Who previously accepted the hardships of practice,
And now bears the full weight of the vehicle.

For the sake of dharma slash through hardships!
Hold tight to the seat of your courage!
See through to the core of primal void!
Understand there is nothing to meditate at all!

Do not be distracted for even a moment!
Reduce attachment to all your experiences!
Do not speak of your realization to others!
Preserve the ability to stay by yourself!

Do not be distracted by social exchanges!
Reduce obsession with food!
Decrease attachment to possessions!
Decrease painful longing for friends!

Reduce hatred for enemies!
Be impartial toward companions!
Do not seek alms if you do not need them!
Do not discourage the faithful!

Do not sell instructions for money!
Never reject poor vessels of dharma!
Do not behave pretentiously!
Do not pointlessly reveal your signs of achievement!

Reduce deceit and empty boasting!
Never empower those unworthy of dharma!
Develop the worthy with method!

Never show off in front of a crowd!
Do not criticize your superiors!
Do not despise your inferiors!
Never cease praying day and night!

Take refuge in the Triple Gem!
Cultivate love and compassion!
Work for the welfare of others, whatever they do!
Dedicate your achievements, pray for others!
Purify the three conceptual spheres![45]
Seek attainments with the seal of reality!

After this song "father" and "son" went into retreat together at Lachi.

Mila Reveals His Attainment

While Jetsun was staying at Chu Bar, a strong relationship developed between himself and Geshé Neusurpa.[46] Although they had never met face to face, they had developed a great friendship from afar due to their mutual respect.

Once, after Neusurpa had given the vow of functional mind-for-enlightenment[47] to one of his disciples, he told him, "If you wish to meet a buddha, go see Jetsun Milarepa." So the disciple set out, bearing a package of tea as an offering, in the company of a disciple of Geshé Jen Ngapa[48] who was going to Nepal to procure ritual implements.

When they arrived they offered the tea to Mila and said, "Having heard of your reputation, great Jetsun, we have traveled a long way to see you. Please touch our hearts with dharma."

Mila replied, "You, disciple of Jen Ngapa, are lying. Procure your ritual implements, offering cups, and so on, and go on your way. But to you who was sent by my good friend Neusurpa, I will of course teach dharma."

Jen Ngapa's disciple was much deflated, it is said. Then Jetsun asked them, "You are both central Tibetans—are there said to be any siddhas in the central province of Ü?"[49]

Jen Ngapa's disciple said, "One man named Nyen Mi Samden is a siddha because he is served food by local spirits." In response Mila sang:

> Homage to the feet of my father lama.
>
> Those possessed by spirits,
> Those involved in conjuring and such—

Of course they eat spirit food;
View rocky, snowy mountains,
Springs, and forests as delightful abodes;
And see spirit traps and implements[50]
As garments and enjoyable things.
I have heard that they even take their share
Of flesh from those with weakened life force.

Seben Repa asked, "Jetsun, have you ever eaten spirit food?"
"Not just a few times, but many," replied Mila. He then sang:

Homage to the feet of my lama.

The various human foods,
After conversion to pure nectar,
Become continual nectar offerings
To the divine mandala of my body.

Likewise, the "spirit food" of nonperception of identities,
Converted to untainted nectar
Through the power of illusionary magic,
Becomes an offering to the appearance-void deity.

And freedom from hunger, thirst, and craving for food,
Through the mental magic of concentration,
Becomes freedom from all affliction,
For it is the dakini's food itself.

Jen Ngapa's disciple spoke again, "Geshé Jen Ngapa sees the face of his personal deity and receives dharma from him. He has thus attained both ordinary and supreme siddhis."[51]
So again Mila sang:

Homage to the feet of my lama.

I rejoice at his attainment of both siddhis.
By seeing his personal deity's unveiled face,

He knows that all things in the superficial world
Appear, yet are not absolutely real.

Having seen mind's nature
And cleared away the fog of ignorance,
Even dakinis show him their faces.
In the realm of reality they teach him dharma
Concerning one's own natural purity and clarity,
Without perception of identities,
Beyond views and thoughts.

You have not listened and thought about your lama's words.
The dakinis prophesied that in this life
He would achieve all desired siddhis,
Both ordinary and supreme.

The disciple wondered to himself, "From the way this lama praises dakinis, has he seen the faces of any tantric deities other than dakinis?" But Mila again sang:

Homage to the feet of my lama.

Listen, monk of Ü:
On the level of absolute reality
The unborn, unceasing, space-like state
Is inexpressible, inconceivable, transcending thought.

On the level of the superficial world
If you wish to see the faces of personal deities,
Look here, you two young monks:

He pulled aside his robe, and they saw his channels of currents and his five centers with deities such as Samvara, Hevajra, Guhyasamaja, and all the others dwelling therein. Struck with faith and awe, they requested dharma and, after receiving the series of initiations, were able to gain a foothold on the path.

Aids to Illumination

Returning to the highlands of Upper Tibet, the great Jetsun went to Jarasa of Drin. Spreading a coarse woolen mat inside the hollow of a rotten tree, he took up residence there. When Drigom Lingkhapa came to see him, Mila sang him a song of the aids, or favorable conditions, for illumination.

Eh Ma! This desolate forest is bliss!
This core of the holy path is bliss!
A place where Conquerors find enlightenment,
Abounding with flowers and fruit,
Where trees sway like dancers,
Where monkeys sport,
A place resounding with the calls of birds,

Living alone in this desolate place,
I am happier than happy;
Avoiding social affairs, completely happy!

A body free from heat and cold is bliss,
But glowing with tummo heat is great bliss!

Breath free from in- and out-flow is bliss,
Absence of conversation is bliss,
But forgetting speech is greater bliss!

Unconcern with cleanness of food is bliss,
Total freedom from preconception is even better.

Lack of possessiveness is bliss,
Lack of possessions is even better.

Concentration neither excited nor depressed is bliss,
But clarity of the natural mind is even better.

Meditation in a desolate forest is bliss.
This coarse woolen mat beneath me is bliss.
This robe of Nepali cotton is bliss to my body.
This food of meditation is bliss to my stomach.
Thought-free concentration is bliss to my mind.

In winter this forest is bliss.
In summer a mountain cascade is bliss.

This is my yogin's way of practice.
All expert meditators following after
Should take up practice this way.

If you fear repetitive life in the three realms,
Practice dharma without regret
Even in the face of death.

Milarepa in Lhasa

Mila went on to Lhasa and completely circled the city. Afterwards, he mingled with the crowd in a large bazaar. From among a group of young women there, one exclaimed, "Is this a barbarian from Unisu? What kind of man *is* he?"

Another said to him, "Sing us a song, if you know how." So Mila sang this song:

> I pray for blessings from my lamas,
> Siddhas of the lineage
> Extending from great Vajradhara
> Down to Translator Marpa.
>
> Upon sun-moon thrones on the crown of my head
> Sit the lamas of the Oral Lineage.[52]
> If an example be made,
> They are like pearls strung on silken thread.
> I am inspired with faith in my lamas' blessings.
>
> The Triple Gem is my support.
> If an example be made,
> Such undistracted protection
> Is like an infant tended on mother's lap.
> Thus freed from worry, my mind is happy.
>
> On my right warriors transmit their blessings.
> If an example be made,
> Such removal of obstructive conditions

Is like a sharp weapon turning to the brain.[53]
Freed thus from obstruction, my mind is happy.

On my left heroines transmit their blessings.
If an example be made,
Such bestowers of both types of siddhis
Are like the circle of mother, sisters, and lovers.
With all needs thus provided, my mind is happy.

Oath-bound dharma protectors gather before me.
If an example be made,
Such attendance through oath-bound service
Is like charging servants with work.
With every wish provided for, my mind is happy.

I have perfected the three skills for seeing reality.
If an example be made,
Such superiority over the Lesser Vehicle
Is like a lion striding across snow mountains.
Thus freed from anxiety, my mind is happy.

In meditation I spread the wings of method and wisdom.
If an example be made,
Such flight through the sky of reality
Is like a vulture soaring high in the air.
Freed thus from fear of falling, my mind is happy.

Force of practice propels my mind.
If an example be made,
This hunter who ensnares depression and inertia
Is like a striped tiger roaming the jungle.
Thus freed from fear, my mind is happy.

I have realized the resultant triple body.
If an example be made,
Such emanated bodies providing for the welfare of beings
Are like goldfish darting about in a pond.
Freed thus from self-doubt, my mind is happy.

I am singing a short song of realization.
If an example be made,
Such triumph over appearances
Is like a dragon's roar resounding through space.
Freed thus from discouragement, my mind is happy.

I, the yogin Milarepa,
Wander empty mountains aimlessly.
If an example be made,
I am like an antelope living in the mountains.
Freed thus from fear, my mind is happy.

I have realized equanimity free from conceptual patterning.
If an example be made,
I am like an infant without discursive thought.
Freed thus from troubles, my mind is happy.

In this way I have achieved bliss.
You god-like humans—especially you young women
Standing and strolling around this market—
Turn your sight inward, into your minds,
And practice without fear even in the face of death.

May all beings without exception
Attain the exalted state of buddhahood.

All present were struck with admiration, and many came forth to receive dharma-connection. Mila found an abundance of alms among them. This was the story of Mila's visit to the city of Lhasa.

Appearances and Mind: Tips for Practicing Mahamudra

While the great Jetsun was living in Chu Bar, Shengom Repa approached him and asked, "Precious Lama, are all these appearances merely mental?" Milarepa replied:

I bow to the feet of my lama.

Appearances are the mind's voice.
Silenced or not,
You should realize their natural clarity.

Patternings are the mind's music.
Silenced or not,
You should realize their natural clarity.

This illusory body is the mind's support.
Whatever its unchanging essence,
You should arrive at tranquil bliss.

Inner voices are the cause of distraction.
Clear them in the voiceless, thoughtless state.

Dualistic thought is the mind's enemy.
Strive for the goal: freedom from concepts.

Freedom from dualism is the mind's friend.
Make it shine in the birthless, deathless state.

The dharma-body is the mind's ripe fruit.
Nurture it in the state beyond words and concepts.

At another time, Lo Repa approached him. After paying respects and offering a mandala, he asked:

I greet my lama who knows all three times,
With admiration in body, speech, and mind.

I, repa of Lo, with slight experience,
Have met with you, great siddha.
Although my knowledge of things is small,
I make this request of my reverend lama
With strong desire, determination, and respect:
Endow my mind with blessings and ability.

By previously requesting the means of seeing,
I have seen a bit of my mind's reality.
Now kindly grant me the method of its development.

Mila sang this song in reply:

I pray to the feet of my lama.

Listen, son, young Lo Repa:
This old man will not last much longer
So I will now impart my ultimate message;
Bear it well in mind, Lo Repa.

Although there are many means for clearing
These superficial, illusory appearances,
In the production stage one's apparent body
Is like a rainbow, reflected as the deity.
In the appearance-void state of the deity's body,

One enjoys one's fill of food and drink;
This is achieved when free from attachment.

In the completion stage, after gradually drawing
The animate and inanimate
Into the deity's clear-light body
Focus on the nada-sound;[54]
And when nada itself becomes very refined
The yogin is focused in freedom from patterning
Through the media of the four propositions.[55]

This is the actual state of mahamudra;
Thus, abide in the import of this statement:
"Here there is nothing at all to clarify,
Not the slightest concentration object.
Reality, when really viewed,
When really seen, is liberation."[56]

Further, on that occasion Drigom Repa, Shiwa ö, Tag Gom Repa, and others asked him, "Precious lama, several spiritual teachers have said that our mahamudra practice is nihilistic. Is this so?"
Jetsun replied:

I pray to the feet of my lama.

Though you have realized the birthless nature of things,
Do not deny the reality of cause and effect.

Though in the state of ceaseless enjoyment-body,
Do not deny the superficial world.

Though dwelling in the natural state,
Do not deny the production stage.

Again, Dro Pen Trashi and others asked him, "Precious lama, because you have grown old in body, please give us your 'ultimate precepts'."
Mila then repeated the preceding song of precepts and added these verses in conclusion:

Until phenomena and mental reality are unified,
Do not deny cause and effect.

Until consciousness is imbued with wisdom,
Do not disparage tranquilization practice.

Until tranquilization and insight are integrated,
Do not disparage the stages of their cultivation.

Until you have confronted the common essence of things,
Do not disparage the wisdoms of learning and thinking.

These precepts of mine,
Well-remembered and practiced,
Will be helpful now and in the future.

Song of Symbols

Once when Mila and Seben Repa were traveling in Upper Nya Nang in the province of Tsang, they visited a village where Mila sang the "Song of the Horned Staff."[57] On that occasion a young villager made this comment about the song: "Wonderful! There is truth in what is said about being able to draw examples from any object. I wish you would sing a song about the symbolic meaning of your cotton robe."

So Mila sang another song:

I remember you Dharma Lord,
How you nurtured me unstintingly
With constant compassion;
Pray make my rough path smooth.

The four-sided cloth of this square robe
Worn by me, the yogin,
Made of soft, white cotton,
Grown from mindless cotton seed
In the lands of India and Nepal,
Indicates the dependent origin of superficial reality.

It was carded by a conscious person,
Taken up on the tips of ten fingers
And spun softly and amply.
It was strung like the continuous warp of compassion
And woven on the loom of ecstasy.

This well-loomed cotton cloth,
When finished, was taken to market
And bought by a wealthy patron,
Who in turn gave it in faith to me.

So now I am dressed in this cotton robe
And it serves me as a reminder:
The four sides stand for the four foci of awareness,
The four main pieces represent the four right efforts,
And the four corners stand for the four bases of miracles—
In all, twelve components of the accumulation path.

Its five-foot length
Includes a lining of four pieces
And three big, central openings
Indicating the seven enlightenment factors;
Penetrative components of the application path.

The eight seams are the Eightfold Superior Path
By which the yogin, striving with awareness,
Completes the meditation path at the ninth stage.

The whiteness of this cotton cloth
Indicates the yogin's pure intent.
And the strength of the cotton signifies
The five powers and five strengths.

Its three-foot width, front and back,
Indicates application to the three doors of action
With undistracted attention in all three times.
Or, in another way, it indicates
Quick compilation of the two stores
By means of the six transcendences.

The softness of this cotton cloth
Symbolizes suppleness and flexibility of mind,
And its frayed edge is a reminder of
The fact that a yogin must also face death.

After its decay it can not be found,
Indicating absorption of the yogin's appearances
Into the state of primal reality-realm.

This cotton robe with such symbolic meaning,
Worn by me, yogin Milarepa,
Is lighter than a feather when I wander the country,
Warmer than a fire when I wander snow mountains,
And more secure than a fort for surviving dangers.
I don't care about the parting of mind and body.

Do you understand this, patrons?

Again, a young patron said, "Very wonderful! But still, would you sing another song about the symbolic meanings of that skull bowl in your hands?" In response, Mila sang this song:

I bow to him who provides welfare for innumerable beings
Radiating uncountable emanated messengers
From untainted, perfect enjoyment-body
Within the perceiverless palace of the reality-body.

Listen again, patron interrogator:
This fine skull food bowl
That I, the yogin, hold in hand
Is from the skull of a most noble man.

His great brain was canopied by a silken skull roof
Indicating the uplifting quality of right view.
The skull roof was supported by its base,

Indicating the climb from low to high through practice.
Within rested his white brain, unmoving,
Indicating the practice of meditation.

To show the cutting of samsara's root
By such view, practice, and meditation,
The skull was cut precisely through the forehead.
To indicate elimination of seeds for both obscurations
It was stripped of skin and flesh.

It is the bone-white color of a conch shell
Due to freedom from the stains of faults and lapses.
Its mouth is upturned to receive the nectar-stream
Of profoundly significant secret mantra;
It is firmly held in the yogin's hand
Out of concern for loss of the three commitments.[58]

Listen yet more, interrogator:
If this skull bowl is considered one piece,
It symbolizes the one-taste of the reality-body.
If it is considered to be three pieces,
It symbolizes indivisibility of the three bodies.

It has the brahmanic aperture
Symbolizing arrival at the state of reality-body.
This marking, like a spreading lineage tree,
Symbolizes arising in the enjoyment-body
In densely packed Akanistha Heaven.
This network of lines like Chinese brocade
Indicates the changing variety of emanation-bodies.

This ridge at the self-spot in back
Indicates victory over the enemy, afflictions,
While lack of one in the frontal empty-spot
Indicates taming of the enemy, egoism.

In the bottom the four teats of the wish-granting cow,
Looking like they were pressed by fingers,
Symbolize provision of all necessities, wants, and dharma;
The lack of vein markings and worm holes
Indicates victory over obstructive evils.

These "elephant-back humps" outside,
Above each ear,
Symbolize pulling the load of the Great Vehicle.
The slight residue here
Indicates that some subtle conceptual patterning remains.

Its form like a lotus petal
Symbolizes freedom from attachment to samsara.
And its smooth, shiny patina
Indicates the warmth of samadhi.

It is held in a yogin's hand
As a sign that he eats the food of the outer world,
Absorbs the food of concentration within,
And is always sustained by nectar,
Untainted in all respects.

These are all merely outer symbols.
The secret inner signs
As explained in Peerless Tantra
Are not fit to be given to you now.

Understand this, fortunate ones!

All the men were struck with strong faith. They requested dharma instruction and offered food, but Mila fasted there for three days and then left.

PART FOUR

ON FEET OF MIRACLES

The Miracles

Mila sometimes used the device of supernormal abilities (siddhis) or "miracles" to demonstrate that the self and world we consider real are actually distortions of reality. He didn't do this often; the wide-eyed reaction of his close disciples in "Meeting with Guru Tsechen" indicates that Mila didn't fly frequently. To think such miracles were merely illusions produced by manipulating the minds of his audience, like a magician's technique of misdirection of attention, is to miss the point. If people are under a spell when perceiving a "miraculous" event, it is equally true that they are under a spell in everyday life—which is an illusion woven from ignorance and conditioned concepts. The ordinary mind is conditioned from birth to misdirect its own attention and perceptions. Seeing Mila levitate and seeing Mila standing on the ground are both interpretations of reality; one is no more miraculous than the other.

We don't normally question the reality of the apparent world. Mila displayed supernormal abilities to create doubt about the tacit assumption that things are as they appear and to induce examination of the habitual mechanisms which pattern ordinary perceptions. Supernormal abilities, such as direct insight into another's mind, also enabled Mila to understand the mind and motivations of his students. And because even the most dedicated students are sometimes discouraged by the enormity of their task, Mila's powers were concrete signs of his development, an inspiration to practice. Such supernormal abilities are a natural consequence of advanced meditation practice, and because they are merely due to alterations of the habitual workings of the mind, they still belong to the realm of appearances. A yogin who fails to understand their superficiality is in danger of becoming fixated on them, or entangled in a conflict between the "real" and "unreal."

Miracles are not always grandiose; they are whatever enabled Mila to survive harsh winters dressed in a thin cotton robe, to live for years on wild herbs, and to communicate his insights to others—even to us, centuries away. "Miracle" is what makes the blessing work, the practice fruitful, the realization break through the masks of appearance. The bodhisattva's vision of the interconnectedness of all life must lie very close to the source of miracle.

Meeting with Guru Tsechen

Chapter 33 of the Hundred Thousand Songs of Milarepa, *mentions that Guru Tsems Chen of La.stod was one of the five enlightened yogins of the time.* Tsems chen *seems to be a variant of brTse.chen ("great love") by which Mila addresses him in this song incorporating several puns on the meaning of "love."*

Milarepa went to Lachi and stayed for a while. At that time a great siddha named Guru Tsechen was living in the region of Upper Tibet, west of Tsang. He was known for his ability to satisfy the spiritual needs of the people. One day Guru Tsechen encountered a monk from central Tibet who had just come from the vicinity of Lachi. The monk had barley cakes and dried meat to share. As the two of them ate the Guru thought, I have heard that the great siddha, Yogin Milarepa, is in the lower country. If only I could meet him even once . . . but I am unable to go down there, and he is not coming here.

He thought awhile longer, then decided, He is a great siddha, equal to a buddha. In his state of concentration he will know my wish. Thereupon he and the monk went to Tisay Mountain.

There Guru Tsechen handed the monk a drum and said, "Beat this." The monk complied and the Guru's thoughts were transmitted on the drum sound.

At that moment, Jetsun was teaching his disciples in Lachi. He suddenly stopped his talk. "Hey, wait a moment. Did you hear that drum sound just now?" he asked.

"We do not hear anything. Where is it coming from?"

"From Tisay, the king of mountains."

"It is impossible that a drum so far away could be heard here. Perhaps it was the wind?"

In reply, Mila sang this song:

I bow at the feet of Marpa Lotsawa,
Precious translator who spoke two tongues,
Whose name resounds like a dragon roar,
Whose sweet song is heard in the ten directions.

I have attained mastery over currents and channels;
I have inner realization of the natural state.
How could a yogin who is like the sky
Be fooled by the external element wind?

I am endowed with six types of super-perception:
When I look and inspect
With super-perception of mind and eye,
I see that on the southeast side of Tisay
The siddha Guru Tsechen
Has handed a drum to a monk who beats it.
The siddha's thoughts are carried on the drum sound.
His words are addressed to me,
And by my super-perception of hearing
I am able to decipher the words I have heard.

The preceding song explains the facts
To all of you gathered here.
This is the message carried on the drum sound:

"Great siddha, repa of the lower country,
I, Yogi Tsechen of the upper country,
Wish to meet you, great siddha.
Please visit this fine place,
You whose mind receives this invitation.

"Please visit, clairvoyant one!
Please listen, clairaudient one!
Please come, miraculous one!
Grant my request, compassionate one!

"Though it is more fitting that I come to you,
Due to circumstances, I am unable.
But in earlier times
In the sugar cane region of India
The faithful woman Magatabhadra,
By kneeling and praying,
Invited Buddha and his circle
To visit from a distant land!"

Mila then concluded his talk, "You must practice according to the meaning of what I have taught you. Meditate undistractedly for three weeks. I will go to Tisay and Seben Repa will come along by holding on to my robe."

At dawn the next day, Seben took hold of the edge of Mila's robe and they flew westward like a pair of geese. Those who remained stared at them wide-eyed and, when they had vanished from sight, fell to the ground in spontaneous prostrations. They returned to their own practice sites and made renewed efforts.

Meanwhile, Jetsun and Seben, who had left Lachi at dawn, arrived at Tisay Mountain with the first direct rays of the sun. On their arrival, Guru Tsechen paid respects, asked for blessings, and said:

You have arrived, great siddha!
Are you well, protector of beings?
How is your health, powerful yogin?
Is your voice clear, Milarepa?
Are you happy, Lord of Dakas?

In reply Milarepa sang this song:

To great Marpa, holy translator,
Precious protector of beings,

Crown of his disciples,
I pray: grant me blessings.

You with "Great Love" for beings,
Is your body mandala unshakable as the earth?
Does the stream of your voice flow like a river?
Is your mind clear like the naturally pure sky?
Do your good qualities grow like a forest?
Do your activities radiate like the sun?

I have come here well-drawn
By the messenger of your thoughts.
I have come well-drawn by your wish,
Carried on the drum's reverberation.

Then Guru Tsechen said, "First we need a place to sit," and he sang:

Appearance is like the sound of a magic drum;
Actually nothing at all can ever be found.
Outwardly, from the viewpoint of appearance,
I will now lay out a place where we can sit."

Saying this, with his bare hands, he carved an excellent cave out of solid rock, big enough for six people. Thereupon Jetsun sang:

In this empty cave of birthlessness
I write the clear, unceasing seed-syllable "Ah"
And do constant, unbridled worship.
May all be freed from samsara
Realizing the birthless essence of "Ah."

On the wall of the cave a white letter "Ah" was clearly visible. It exists even today, and the cave is known as the "Ah Cave."
Guru Tsechen then said, "Now please bless this place I have provided. Tell us the story of the geographical formations from which these snow mountains evolved." So Jetsun sang:

I bow to Translator Marpa's feet.
He knew and told the history
Of how the worldly realms evolved,
Especially Tibet, land of snowy peaks.
This lama told of the mountains,
Tisay and Kang Jen,
Two among many regal mountains found
Beneath the canopy of Buddha's speech.

In each of these two mountains
Lives a most superior man.
Kingly Mount Tisay is best,
Like the pure white butter of the gods.

It stands at the head of four rivers.[59]
To the east lies the step-mountain of scented herbs,
To the south, beneath a golden cliff,
Swirls turquoise Lake Manasarovar,
The peak of Royal Mountain lies to the west,
And the golden expanse of Indigo meadow is to the north.

Between these compass points are located
The forest "King of Medicinal Herbs,"
The lake where Prince Norbusang washed,
The abode of five-hundred yakshas,
And other foothills, meadows, and valleys.
At the center, surrounded by foothills
As if attended by ministers, sits regal Tisay.

To worldly eyes
It appears as I have described,
But for students of the path
This Tisay, king of snows,
Is the vast mansion of Chakrasamvara;
A mandala of the body and its environment.

This royal peak, supreme method,
Is embraced by the lesser peak, wisdom goddess.

It is cleft by three geoformations,
The valleys Lha, Dar, and Dsong,
Symbols of the three channels ida, pingala, and susuma.

The sixteen wisdom-goddesses live there
In gesture of worshipful offering,
And the four door guards, like the raven-headed
Live, keeping watch over the four entrances.

They appear like this
To yogins who practice mantra,
But in the sight of persons
Following the basic Vehicle
The Superior Yenlag Jung
Sits holding fly-whisk and incense pot
In the resplendent interior
Of this royal snow-mountain.

Thirteen-hundred arhats surround him;
Innumerable bodhisattvas, disciples,
And self-buddhas sit
Offering them continual worship.

To the naked eye of worldly beings
Footprints of Muni and arhats are clearly seen,
As are three peaks imbued with blessings—
The abodes of three families of protectors.
The self-formed stone images of Chakrasamvara,
Vajrapadma, and four-armed Mahakala
Are there, replete with offerings in stone.

In the sight of Hindus
There are many Hindu stone formations
Like those resembling Samantabhadra
And Vajrapadma, the Linga abode
Of great Siva himself,
And even Hanuman, the monkey king,
Rendering service to Manjusri.

151

These geoformations can also be seen
According to the system of the western Bönpos.
But for yogins who have seen essential reality
All these are mere elaborations on voidness.
Yet, until superficial appearances are cleansed,
They do exist in an illusory way.
So do not deny superficial reality
With the empty speech of one who's not seen reality.

So I now offer illusory, but sincere, respects
To the host of peerless yoga deities,
To this superior man with his circle,
And to the protectors and guardians of teaching
Who live on this royal mountain.

I offer worship, confess my sins,
And rejoice in the virtue of others.
I pray you remain forever turning the wheel of dharma,
And I dedicate everything for the benefit of beings.

I offer this melodic worship
And share this feast of song
With lama, personal deities, and Triple Gem.

Jetsun and his disciple Seben remained there three weeks, discussing
dharma extensively. The monk received the blessings of both siddhas and
was able to cut off the effects of former action. He became a siddha himself,
detached from interest in this life. At another time during their stay, Jetsun
sang this song:

I bow at the feet of Marpa of Lhodrak
Precious, holy protector of beings.

Guru with great love for beings—
In the great state of unwavering bliss
Within the palace of pure reality-element,
Resides your illusory body, unshakable.

May you quickly arrive at Akanistha Heaven,
Your emanated bodies streaming to every trainee's place
From your enjoyment-body to provide help for others,
While remaining rooted in the reality-body palace of your own
    welfare.

Jetsun and Seben then returned to the lower country, traveling for three days. There his disciples greeted him with a circle of ceremonial offerings and asked, "Did you meet the great siddha of the highlands?" Mila replied in song:

Siddha Guru Tsechen
And I, Yogin Milarepa,
Met on the neck of snow-white Tisay.

We displayed physical emanations,
And conversed in voice-streams—
Two minds flowing together in the reality-sphere.

Because of this we penetrated reality,
Realizing the illusory and dreamlike.
Settled comfortably in great bliss,
Mingling in equanimity,
Peacefully resting in the state of reality,
We moved through the evanescent, superficial world
With unexpressible reality, free of fabrication.

Mila Saves a Dying Boy

Bön is the shamanistic religion native to Tibet. Following the advent of Buddhism in that country the two religions vied for the faith and patronage of the people. As the Bönpos assimilated Buddhist ideas the of scope of Bön was gradually broadened. The Buddhists, as well, adapted Bön-po techniques of communicating with the Tibetan peoples. A rivalry for the people's patronage and zeal was well under way by Milarepa's time, as indicated in this story. Mila is emphatic in delineating the validity and advantages of the Buddhist system of practice.

After spending the winter at Lachi, the great lord of yogins went to Drin and Nya Nang in the summer. Arriving in the village of Gelay in Nya Nang, he found that the beloved only son of a rich man named Namkha Wangchuk lay ill and near death. All the Bön priests of Drin and Nya Nang had been summoned to perform curative services such as mantra recitation and soul-ransoming.[60] However, these priests were ineffective and the boy remained near death.

Namkha Wangchuk approached Mila, paid respects, and asked, "Precious lama, my only son will die before reaching manhood. Please help his mind onward with your transference blessings."[61]

Jetsun went inside and gave his blessings with slurred, jumbled speech. He remained in concentration for a long time, and then said, "Bring me water." From that point on Mila was able to speak correctly. He gave the boy the ritual ablution of Usnisavijaya and the blessings of the Goddess Kurukulla.[62]

154

After nightfall the boy improved somewhat, so his father prepared an elaborate feast which he offered to Jetsun. As he was offering the Bön priests their share of the reward, the head priest commented, "Ascetic Milarepa, we Mantric Bönpos performed many rituals: exorcism, soul-ransom, drawing back the life-force, reversal of circumstances, and the like. Your blessings and invocation of fortune were useless to the sick boy." The Bönpo priest followed this up with a song, after which he said, "Why doesn't the ascetic yogin also compose a song?"

So Mila sang this song:

> I bow to the feet of my triple-bodied lama
> Whose clouds of compassion pervade the limits of space,
> Letting fall a constant rain of blessings,
> Easing the hot torment of the afflictions and five poisons.
> Bless me with natural freedom from clinging.
>
> These illusory appearances exist from beginningless time;
> However you treat them, you are still trapped by afflictions:
> Seeking a path to freedom, but wandering in samsara,
> Meditating the natural state, but bound by chains of
>   extremism,
> Treading the path, but burdened by the eight worldly
>   concerns,
> Vowed to enlightenment, but polluted by partiality,
> Possessing the four empowerments,
> But blind to the subtle path's essence.
> Oh, compassion for deluded beings!
> I myself remain focused in unspeakable reality.

Again, the Bön priest spoke up: "The common saying, 'a talkative mouth is sure to be fed,' certainly applies here. This sick boy of the Dor Shag clan was cured by the nine-fold method of our Bön religion. By mere coincidence you came here and appeared to help. This great respect and offering directed at yourself is due only to your clever mouth. Actually you do not even know the Bön practice of attracting good fortune and prosperity; you are not even able to rig just one type of spirit trap. Your statement about your 'unspeakable' practice is certainly correct."

Jetsun thought, "I do not need to argue with these debased Bönpos. But

155

so that people will be receptive to other dharma practitioners in the future, I should give some reply." So he sang this song:

> To my compassionate lama, skilled in method,
> I pray with intense admiration and respect,
> Bless me to work for the welfare of myself and others.

> Bön teachers who cannot control their own apparent nature
> Claim to control the devils of mind and body!
> They claim to mend the broken life-force and vitality
> Of a fatally ill boy.

> Actually you are like greedy children
> Who clutch their possessions tightly.
> You mutter nonsense like drunkards,
> Wind woolen threads round your heads like spindles,
> And beat your battered drums like performers.

> You guzzle dark beer like fish,
> Shameless in all behavior like a depraved ruler,
> You greedily stuff alms bags like bandits.
> In airing all these things
> I must be restrained or you will become enraged.

> I am the yogin who controls appearances.
> With great love I gather many spirit traps
> In the illusory vessel of void appearances.
> With great compassion I moisten this vessel with nectar,
> Bless it with the four infinitudes,
> And with the four social means[63] I attract malevolent spirits.

> In the torma-vessel of unborn voidness
> I prepare the torma[64] of brilliant wisdom
> To delight the gods of unconditioned gnosis
> And appease all malevolent spirits—
> Holders of karmic debts and blood-hatreds.

That is my story in accord with Bön;
Now here is my story in accord with dharma.

I, the yogin Milarepa,
Climbed from low to high with subtle practice,
Swooped from high to low with perfect view.

I made firm the foundation of faith,
Built a fine house with windows of introspection,
Supported it with pillars of great vigor,
Correctly opened the doorways of gnosis,
And erected the stairways to higher states and freedom.

Within its broad and ample interior
I lay on my side of four right efforts;
On the four cushions of the foci of awareness.
My throne was supported by the four "feet" of miracles.[65]

Developed in physical strength of the five powers
And endowed with the perfect confidence of five strengths
I, the yogin well-adorned
With the seven enlightenment factors
And eight branches of the noble path,
Restored the almost exhausted breath
Of this rich patron's son
With profound blessings and fortuitous invocation.

From the space realm of reality I pulled
Back his life functions right before they were lost
And stabilized them with the profound blessings
Of goddess Usnisavijaya
And saviouress Kurukulla.

Rest easy in your minds
About my reward for doing this,
Though I was given valuable possessions

I possess the wealth of inner satisfaction;
I do not need such worldly wealth.

If you wish to repay me for this kindness
Abandon the ten evils, such as killing,
And cultivate the ten virtues' bounty.

Striving hard for virtue while compiling the stores,
It is best to eliminate insistence;
Eliminate attachment to essenceless samsara.

Give away possessions, food, and wealth
To accrue such enjoyables in later life.
Preserve morality to obtain higher birth
By occasional abstinence and cleansing of sin[66]
On the new moon, eighth, and fifteenth days.
These are the causes for higher birth and liberation.

Strive diligently to cultivate patience,
The source for acquiring many good friends
And for obtaining an excellent, auspicious body.
Undertake the struggle for virtuous things with tireless vigor.

If you wish to ingest the food of concentration
It is important to cultivate
The instructions for experience
Received from a qualified lama.

It is important also to examine with the intellect
The Buddha's implicit and explicit, profound and extensive
   sutras
And also the tantras on the natural state.
An auspicious, helpful intent is vital
At all times, in all situations.

I will waste no more time on sweet empty songs,
I, the yogin, will go on my way.

I am always happy to see the faces
Of people who act in accord with dharma.

But they replied, "We are impressed with your words, ascetic yogin. Yet you are firmly attached to the root of egotism. If one should be impartial toward all beings, why do you harbour prejudice in your criticism of us Bönpos? You should practice what you preach!"
So again Mila sang:

To Translator Marpa of Lhodrak
Who nurtures each being like a son
With compassion impartial to all
I pray, grant me blessings.

Bön priests bound with attachment,
Relax your minds and consider this:

The omniscient, inoffensive Buddha's
Teaching concerning the natural state
Is partial and prejudiced only about
Evildoers and the three lower realms.

By revealing samsara's inner nature
He established the true path,
As parents who fear their children's straying
Will beat and scold them
To guide them on the right way.

Of all gods and spirits of the apparent world
Shenrab,[67] so respected by yourselves,
Praised some and disparaged others;
Some are worshipped with meat and beer,
Others are thrown burnt leavings in the street.

The excuse for acting thus
Toward spirits equally deserving
Is that some are endowed with power,
While others are weak and ineffective.

159

Likewise, I will explain the reason
For my partiality and prejudice
While making statements to you,
Who cannot bear your own state:

Nonbuddhists, in teaching "truth,"
Lead people into lies;
Buddha, in teaching lies,
Leads people to truth.

Your teacher Shenrab, in works
Such as the *White Serpent Compendium*,
Sets forth your ultimate tenet:
One attains enlightenment
In the mandala of the five serpent gods!
You should consider well
That nagas are numbered among the animals.

Unable to bear your wrong ideas
I let slip just a few words.
At this you became enraged.
There is no sense in heaping more bad action
On to what is already unproductive.
Forgive me if I struck a sore spot.

At this they were confused. One young Bönpo paid respects to Jetsun, placed Jetsun's feet on his head and made confession. He abandoned the Bön religion and worldly affairs and practiced the profound path of great teachings, Naropa's six yogas, and so on. He is said to have become a great yogin, a master of the apparent world.

Jetsun remained for several days at the request of Namkha Wangchuk and his circle of friends, teaching them dharma. He also gave many more initiations and blessings to the sick boy who had recovered. Though offered many things, Mila did not accept them. Saying, "I am going to wander the desolate valley of Lachi," he went on his way. This was the great repa's song on the debased Bön religion.

Mila Guides His
Mother's Spirit

After death and before rebirth each thread of events which we call a living
being *continues its existence as what is loosely termed a* mental being, or
consciousness principle. *This state of existence is called the* bardo, *and the
continuation of the being is called* bardo voyager *or* bardo being. *According-
ing to tradition, during the seven weeks of bardo the consciousness principle
undergoes intense and unusual experiences—a mental playing-out of the
residues of the past life's attitudes and behavior.*[68] *Tibetans believe that
realized beings can direct the events of the bardo in order to gain the rebirth of
their choice and, in addition, may influence the bardo consciousness of others
so as to affect their rebirth.*

This story is also related in the Hundred Thousand Songs of Milarepa
*(Chapter 54, pp. 615–19), although in a very different style. The present
song corresponds to Mila's two songs to his sister Peta (pp. 619–21). The
occasion of his finding and meditating on his mother's bones is told in his
autobiography (Evans-Wentz, pp. 174–75).*

Once the master Yogin sang a song to a group of Bönpos about the
guiding of a dead man's consciousness. Afterwards his sister Peta
broke into tears, saying, "When our old mother died there were no services,
not even someone to offer just one torma." Mila replied in song:

I pray to my kind father.

Listen, Peta Gonkyitma,
Our old mother's box of a body
Exhausted the momentum of its life force.
Illusory mind and body parted,
Her consciousness roamed the bardo leading to rebirth.

By force of bad action she strayed to low realms,
But afterwards I, the yogin, arrived
And, head cushioned on her dead body's bones,
Remained seven days in concentration.

Into the vessel-mansion where
Peerless tantra deities abide in seven groups
I drew her with concentration, mantra, and mudra,
And after cleansing with mantra, removed her.

I conferred complete blessings and fourfold empowerment,
And, after clearing obscurations of mind,
Revealed mahamudra to her.
She has now moved on to higher realms.

That is how I performed the seven-week rite
For the mother who bore our bodies and minds.

All present were very impressed. They offered respects and circled Jetsun.

Song over a Dog's Corpse

One warm day Jetsun was traveling on the great Pel Thang plateau when he came upon the corpse of a dog covered with a mass of maggots. Moved by compassion, he sat down beside the corpse with concentrated mind.

Three days later a group of traders from the pasture lands arrived and told Jetsun that they had been traveling through the Nga Ri Valley. One of them asked, "Yogin, what are you doing sitting beside this rotten dog's corpse?"

Jetsun replied, "Crows were about to eat the maggots on this corpse, so I am guarding it."

"You can not guard it forever. Better just to leave it."

Another added, "You have no provisions, not even any clothes. Where do you plan to go?"

Mila replied, "I have no plan to go; I have just arrived."

"Where did you come from?"

"I came from the direction of Nga Ri Valley."

"We also just came from the direction of Nga Ri, but we did not see you. How long have you been here?"

"I have been sitting here for three days."

"You do not seem to need any food—that is surprising. Are you a siddha? If so, please teach us some dharma."

So Jetsun sang this song:

> I pray at the feet of my father-lama.
>
> Wandering the illusory plain of the six states of being,
> Taking up illusory bodies of birth, death and bardo,

Passing through cities of bardo and dream,
I've traveled the narrow path between existence and bardo.

I have lived over and over in hell regions,
Been tormented by neurotic hunger and thirst,
Experienced the miserable stupidity of animals,
And merely tasted the lives of humans and gods.

Now by chance I have obtained human life.
In youth I employed evil mantric powers
And came to regret it enormously.

I then went to Marpa, best of men,
At his "monastery" in Lhodrak.
Guided by that great siddha
I made my human existence meaningful.

Having no wealth to offer, I offered service
Of body and speech as far as I was able
And especially the worship of my practice.

Through the key of such practice
I obtained mastery of currents and channels;
Thus, I have no fear of physical disease.

The bliss-warmth of tummo burns in my body;
Thus, I've no fear of snow, rain or wind.

I eat the food of taintless concentration;
Thus, I've no fear even of famine.

Always in the company of enlightenment-mind,
I place no faith in feeble companions.

I spend my winter months in mountain retreats,
Eating the roots of mountain herbs
In the company of friendly mountain deer.

I spend the spring midst rocks and ravines,
Eating nettles and wild leeks,
Kept company by friendly foxes and blackbirds.

Summer months are spent on cliffs and snow mountains,
Eating pebbles and drinking streams for support;[69]
Flocks of white vultures serve as friends.

In autumn I beg for food,
Seeking common food like a bird;
Realized beggars serving for friends.

I am hard to meet, so stay here happily.

The traders were struck with strong faith and said, "Our village is nearby. Will you visit for a few days?" They pressed him repeatedly until Jetsun replied, "If you will not listen to me and stay here, I will come in three days."

He remained by the corpse for three more days, guiding the dog's consciousness to a higher state of existence and establishing a karmic connection with the maggots. Then, early in the morning of the third day, a man came to guide him to the village. Jetsun stayed there for several days teaching dharma. They begged him to stay permanently, but he declined and went on to the great Lachi snow mountain. This is the story of guiding the dog's consciousness upward, together with a song.

The Yogini's Dream

Once while Jetsun was staying at the great Stone Canopy Cave of Lachi, the yogini Darbum Chödrön arrived with yogini Drub Chungma Leggyen. After they made elaborate offerings and paid respects many times, Darbum sang:

> Homage to you, precious saviour of beings.
> I pray to you who are so kind.
> I take refuge in you, compassionate one.
> Pray protect me with great mercy.

> I, Darbum Chödrön,
> Prayed to you four times each day,
> Then instigated the enlightenment-mind
> With constant, undistracted attention.

> This morning at first light
> In a vision while asleep
> I flew high into the sky
> And traveled toward the rising sun.

> There, in a land of lapis-lazuli,
> Comfortable and soft as the palm of my hand,
> I saw a lake, clear and sparkling,
> A wondrous tree of many jewels,
> Deer playing with abandon,
> Peacocks, parrots, and water birds,
> Delightful thickets of grouse—
> All in profusion staggering the imagination.

In the midst of that land,
Covered with fragrant flowers
Like a cloak upon the earth,
Stood a delightful palace.
Square, with four doors and porches,
Eighty-four thousand pillars rose up
Within that spacious mansion
Fashioned from seven types of gem.

And in that palace's vast chamber,
Upon a throne of jewels and fine silk
Supported by two fearless lions,
Sat the royal Conqueror Akshobya,[70]
Teaching his numberless circle.

From the edge of the audience
I tossed a handful of flowers,
Then knelt with folded hands and listened,
Memorizing the words and meanings
Of the twelve-fold chain of dependent occurrence
Both forwards and backwards.
After paying homage, I left.

To one side of that palace
Sat another mansion, fine and gracious.
Within, a host of dakinis,
Beautiful of form in the flush of youth
And adorned with jeweled ornaments,
Performed various songs and dances.

They raised a broad throne of seven jewels,
Canopied it with fine silks,
Anointed it with sweet-scented water,
And adorned it with many flowers.

Some held fragrant incense burners,
Some held parasols and victory banners,
Some held musical instruments,

Some waved silk banners in the sky,
And some proclaimed this invitation:

"We invite you, Pelden Shaypa Dorje,[71]
Supreme lord of all dakinis,
Son born of the heart
Of royal conqueror Akshobya."

But some said, "It is too soon
To invite the Lord of Dakinis;
We should go to Jetsun ourselves
To see him and offer homage."

They departed and I awoke,
Body sweating and heart beating fast.
Thus I came into Jetsun's presence
To make this statement before my lama:

May we have the auspicious circumstance
Of your continued presence here on earth,[72]
Cutting through the mental doubts
Of ourselves, the ocean of disciples,
And of all practitioners, present and future.

May the mountain of your body be firm,
The stream of your speech flow far,
And your mind abide unwaveringly
In the state of reality.

May the brilliance of your reality-body
Burn bright in the palace of Chu Bar,
Your voice expound profound dharma,
And your mind abide forever
In the primordial state.

May the bee-like swarm of yogin-disciples
Savor the profound dharma nectar of your speech.

Sweet fragrance streaming
From the lotus garden of your body.

Then the great Jetsun said, "Listen, you two yoginis. In general, all appearances are illusory. Dreams, in particular, are illusory in nature. Your recent dream seems to be only partly prophetic. Because the processes of dream recognition, dream augmentation, dream manipulation, realization of the voidness of dream, and the seeing of innumerable Buddha realms in dreams are so complex,[73] your recent vision of Conqueror Akshobya's Buddha realm is only partial. And although the dakinis may call me, I will most likely remain a few more years.

"Yoginis, such a vision was due to the force of your purification of karmic obstructions. However, if you believe any such dream-vision to be real, you have fallen under the influence of the divine devil.[74] You should remain clear in the state of reality." He followed this with a song:

Reality-body, realm of purified conceptual patterns;
Enjoyment-body, treasury of auspicious signs and marks;
Emanation-body, revealed to a multitude of trainees—
The three spontaneous bodies of Teacher Marpa.
Please sit like an ornament on the crown of my head.

Through beginningless time this deluded mind
Has appeared to the unrealized as illusory samsara.
But for those focused in the state of reality,
It is appearance-voidness, clarity-voidness, bliss-void
   mahamudra.

Like filling a crystal vase with water,
The naturally aware, clear and brilliant reality-body
Is free from materialism or nihilism regarding birth and death.
For one who has realized this state
Even the terms "birth" and "death" do not apply.

I, the yogin, have experienced this;
Sisters, you should experience it, too.
We are sure to meet in the purified realm
By seeing the illusoriness of void appearances.

Do not view the dream visions
As real, yoginis.

Eliminate attachment to
Inherently painful samsara, yoginis.

See the deluded affairs of the immature
To be illusion, yoginis.

Bear in mind the precepts
Given by this lama, yoginis.

Focus yourselves on the explicit goal
Of mahamudra, yoginis.

I, the yogin Milarepa,
Applied the precepts without leaving my cushion
Until realization of the actual state dawned within.

When voidness and cognition were inseparably united,
I realized the equivalence of earth and gold
And the inseparable equality of beings and buddhas.
For such a yogin as myself
What can be said of "birth" and "death?"

However, in view of your fervent prayer
May my life continue inexhaustibly,
And thereby may good fortune continue
For the sake of those overcome with delusion.

May the minds of my worthy disciples
Be satisfied by dharma,
And their basic awareness[75] be transformed into gnosis
Naturally providing for beings' welfare
Through a continual succession of disciples.

I offer this song of worship, Triple Gem!
Share in this feast of sound, host of dakinis!
Remove obstructive conditions, nonhumans!
Attend this auspicious song of worship!

Darbum Chödrön and all others present rejoiced in delight. This was the song of the three means of continued presence.

The Great Fire

The great Jetsun announced that he and Shengom Repa would travel to the Nepali District.[76] Along the way a fire broke out on a large mountain. Because the path was very narrow, with no escape above or below, Mila realized they were trapped. A huge cloud of smoke descended and made the day seem like dusk. Sitting down, he said to Shengom Repa, "Sit next to me and grab hold of my hand," then he cried out, "oh, young repa, if you have any realization, now is the time you need to use it! No matter how clever you are in giving a hundred or a thousand explanations of dharma, if you have not grasped their essence you are no different than a parrot reciting prayers. You should focus your mind in the primordial voidness of reality." Mila remained seated.

Later that day the young repa looked up. His lama was asleep amidst tongues of flame, red and black, while on the other ridges the fire had died out. The young repa felt cold as he looked his lama over, wondering if he had been harmed by the fire. But Mila's robe was not even singed, and in astonishment Shengom sang:

> Precious kind lama,
> Lying within the blazing fire
> Like the king of the fierce wisdom gods,
> Is this illusion or is this real?
> Is this true or is it false?
>
> This demonic obstruction
> Was viciously committed against the holy;

In this respect, I am still concerned.

Though around you burns a mass of fire,
Within it your robe remains unsinged—
This fills me with great amazement!
Please rise from the state of reality
And clear away my ignorant doubts.

Then Jetsun woke up within the fire, rose to a squat, and sang this song:

Lama who consumed my mind's obstruction,
Of ripened sins with the blaze of wisdom-fire
Streaming like light rays from your body,
To your feet I bow.

Son, young repa called Shengom,
You of sincere, unbending intent,
You with fervor for pursuing practice,
You so gifted, listen now!

Be at ease, you need not worry;
I have slashed the vine of egoism.
How could harm befall
A yogin awake to the natural state?

This obstruction by the element fire
Set by inhuman demons to harass
Me, the yogin Milarepa,
Burned the grass of this heartless mountain,
Killing many innocent beings.

It destroyed the homes and refuge
Of local gods and serpent spirits,
Scorched this mountainside with fire

Filling sky and air with smoke,
And trapped this yogin within the flames.

Through skill in yogic realization,
When that obstruction arose
I focused my mind just a bit
In the saturative concentration of fire.[77]

By this ability I brought into the path
These illusory, external events.
Superficial appearances may be changed into anything.

Look again, Shengom Repa!
Now my mind is focused
In the saturative water concentration.

Just after the clear melody of his song ended the whole valley filled with water. Floating on its surface, the great Jetsun sang:

Look again, Shengom Repa!
This saturative mandala of wind
Can surely carry off a yogin's mind and body!

They were picked up and blown around Mount Everest and the whole world. Again Mila sang:

Listen again, youthful repa:
Appearances are illusory and false.
All illusory appearances are empty.

If you have not come face to face with this essential reality,
Superficial, false appearances arise from the void;
Thus, it transcends the bounds of being and nonbeing
And is inconceivable, inexpressible.

May we have the fortune of emptying samsara
When everyone realizes this essence.

Then father and son continued their pursuit of accomplishments.

PART FIVE

ULTIMATE PRECEPTS

Expressing the Inexpressible

The goal of buddhist practice is to perceive the true nature of self and world clearly, undistorted by habitual mental patternings. Meditation practice eventually leads to a confrontation of the paradox of the nonduality of the apparent world and the voidness which is its ultimate reality. Teachings concerning this advanced stage of practice are called *ultimate precepts*. Such precepts seem simple, but are subtle and difficult to apply. Like Zen koans, they create a focus of contradiction, a problem whose "solution" requires a profound shift of view which is experienced after intensive effort in practice. Mila's teachings in this section are penetrating and valuable tips for advanced practice. In "The Six Secret Songs," Mila responds to Rechungpa's request for ultimate precepts by exposing his buttocks, covered with calluses from years of sitting in meditation. For Mila, teaching and precept had no significance apart from life itself. Mila's ultimate precepts are not about advancement from the secular to the sacred; rather, they reveal the secular as the sacred it really is.

A basic theme of these precepts is caution concerning the conditioned mind. Any action biased by such conditioning, including spiritual practice, tends to strengthen our bondage to samsara. This is clearly expressed in "Mila's Final Teachings":

On the border between body and mind
The conditioned intellect is the great culprit.
Changing with the flux of ephemeral conditions,
There's no time to realize the unborn meaning.
Keep to the stronghold of the unborn, Rechungpa.

There is a paradox here: freedom from conditioning must be attained through the workings of the conditioned mind itself. The habitual mechanisms which distort our ideas and perceptions must be carefully bridled and analyzed. Because we lack the clarity of unbiased perception, an experienced teacher provides a fulcrum for prying loose the ingrained misperceptions which cause the most assiduous practice to fall short of ultimate realization. Although valuable at earlier stages, scriptural study and meditation practice, as well as well-meant dharma teaching, if biased by conditioned concepts, will not lead to ultimate realization. Because any concept of ultimate freedom is based on conditioned thinking, the teacher must help the student avoid mistaking the experiences of bliss and clarity, which are natural results of meditation, for final realization. At this advanced stage, even dharma can be harmful if misunderstood:

> Somewhere in the unmanifest realm of space
> The perfect buddha is a liar.
> Speaking deceptively of implicit meanings,
> There's no chance to realize the explicit truth.
> Abandon conventional facts, Rechungpa.

On the other hand, Mila had an unquestionable respect for the *potentials* of the human mind, for the inherent capability of all persons to achieve liberation. In these songs there is no doubt about his passion for spiritual development, his fierce pride in his own achievement, and his joy in the advancement of others.

Seben Wants to Build a Shelter

Once while Milarepa was staying in Horse-hoof Cave of Indestructible Red Rock, Seben Repa came to him. After offering respects many times, he asked, "Precious Lama, this place is very conducive to clear awareness and virtuous practice. Others have said they would come, too, but there are no other caves. Should I build a thatched shelter for protection from wind and rain?"

In reply, the lama sang:

> I pray with more than words
> To the dharma intellect of teacher Marpa.
> Lama and personal deity inseparably united,
> Guide me with great compassion.
>
> Oh, yogin named Seben,
> Young repa, listen to me:
>
> To give vital instruction it is necessary to speak,
> But pointless conversation is the source of senseless speech.
>
> While engaged in meditation on a deity,
> Expert meditators do not talk too much.
>
> There is little fault in resting a tired mind,
> But aimless indolence is the root of faults.
> While engaged in mental introspection,
> Expert meditators reduce preconceptions.

It is all right to associate with dharma friends,
But undisciplined friends are the root of evil.
While engaged in solitary practice,
All expert meditators avoid evil friends.

Eat frugally of begged food and alms
According to the situation.
Traveling to beg is a cause of distraction,
Expert meditators stick to their cushions.

Afflictions arise until action is exhausted,
And they lead to conflicts with dharma.
While examining the flow of thought,
Expert meditators correct attachment and aversion.

Keep a few provisions for immediate need;
Hoarding for the future leads to conflict with dharma.
While cutting through the roots of attachment,
Expert meditators reduce attachment.

Find a sleeping place under an overhang;
Building a "mansion" will kill insects needlessly.
While staying in uncertain places such as mountains,
All expert meditators reduce disturbances.

Everyone should have enough food and drink,
But selling knowledge for profit conflicts with dharma.
While relying on the food of austerity,
Expert meditators do not go begging for food.

Everyone should wear a coat against the wind,
But fancy clothes lead to conflict with dharma.
While living the humble life of a beggar,
All expert meditators avoid excessive finery.

Sleeping half the night is good for health,
But addiction to stupefied sleep is like death.

While seeking the goal of the natural state,
All expert meditators avoid deathlike sleep.

There is no fault in ritual feasting when transformed to deity,
But intoxicated celebrants are no different than drunkards.
While cultivating production and completion stages,
Mantric yogins don't crave alcohol.

While cultivating the four ecstasies of the path of method,
Mantric yogins take a gnosis-consort.
But do not take an action-consort
While unable to control in- and out-flow of element.[78]

Bear this is mind, my repa-son.

Mila then said to Seben, "Son, Seben Repa, if you apply yourself assiduously to your share of dharma, the natural state of mahamudra will last day and night, months and years, without break: clear, radiant, ample and relaxed, without hope or fear, free from materialism or nihilism, without coming or going, free from good or bad, free from excellence or fault, free from virtue or sin, without plans or expectations, neither samsara nor nirvana, without activity or unrest, beyond thought, beyond concepts—unmistakable!" Mila once again sang:

Inconceivable, essential state,
Undistracted, unmeditated, inexpressible,
Have you realized it, young repa?

If realized, you would be absorbed in nonduality;
Unrealized, you now make empty talk.
When realized, you will know "buddha" is merely an empty
    word.

The young repa rejoiced and made renewed effort to practice.

A Challenge from Four Ascetics

One day while Jetsun was absorbed in the flowing current of yoga in the Lion Cave of Tag Tsang, four ascetic yogins arrived. They asked him, "Where are you from? When did you come here? You've no possessions—where are they?"

To this interrogation Jetsun replied, "I've come from the region of Nya Nang and have been here about three months. Currently I've no plan to go anywhere. I have no possessions, no hidden wealth to leave behind."

Again they spoke, "This is unprecedented! Anyone who's stayed in this cave for more than a week has died. There's no proof of your stay here. Aren't you lying when you say you've been here for three months? If you're not lying, are you supernatural? We can't believe it. What realization do you have? What kind of accomplishment and verification of experience? Speak truthfully!" In reply Mila sang this song:

> I bow to the feet of Translator Marpa,
> Whose compassion extends to all living beings
> With love for them as for a child,
> Our precious refuge in this life and next.
>
> Since meeting my holy lama
> I've not been accustomed to telling lies.
> Although I do have some realization,
> It's not a topic for worthless discussion.
>
> My solitary life without companions
> Shows that appearances have become my friends.

My living in this empty cave
Shows that pervasive gnosis has dawned.

This thin cotton robe I wear
Signifies the bliss-warmth burning within;
The lack of any carpet beneath me
Shows that I sleep on the bed of reality.

Absence of material possessions
Indicates the satisfaction born within,
And the lack of provisions for survival
Means I survive on the food of meditation.

The absence of even a water jug
Shows that I drink from the stream of enlightenment;
And this little song I sing
Is a sign that realization has arisen within.

My taking appearances as illustrations
Means I know all appearances are illusory;
And this skillful composition of meaningful answers
Indicates that my throat channels have been opened.

Do you catch my meaning, ascetics?
I offer this song of worship, revered lamas.
Share in this feast of sound, host of dakinis.
Remove your obstructions, nonhumans.
Attend this auspicious little song.

Again they said, "You mentioned taking appearances as illustrations. Once when we were in Central Tibet circling Lhasa, a lama-scholar said to us: 'If you are consummate yogins you should be able to take appearances as examples. Sing us a song exemplifying your hat, headband, and damaru-drum.' We were unable, and were derided and laughed at. We still might encounter another such question while wandering the countryside. Could you sing us a meaningful song of examples using this long pointed white hat we wear on our heads, this black twisted headband, and this thin-waisted damaru-drum?" So Mila sang:

Crown of the most skillful,
Best of all translators—
To Great Translator Marpa
I pray for blessings.
Grant me accomplishments, common and supreme.

Now listen, you four companions!
Slash involvement with this mundane life.
Hold fast to the feet of a good lama.
Obtain the precepts—the keys to the profound.
Take up practice with unstinting vigor.
Produce inner realization of the actual state.
Have a heart of compassion and voidness.
Embrace the ultimate goal, the natural state.

When one who knows all appearances and sounds
To be but illusory dreams
Goes seeking alms without discrimination,
Working for the welfare of self and others,
He wears on his head the white yogin's hat
As a sign of his pure overarching view.

The white felt lining
Indicates a mind more supple than wool,
And the white cotton covering represents
The pure intent of mind-for-enlightenment.

These long ear-flaps on either side
Are the mark of profound method and wisdom;
This blue ribbon wound round the edge
Signifies changeless reality.

This mirror fixed in front
Is the sign of ceaseless clear light;
The long, sharp peak is
The mark of sharp discriminating wisdom.

The five colored silks adorning it
Indicate five types of gnosis;
Floral decorations
Mark the attainment of profound empowerment.

The attached artificial braids
Signify concern for the world;
This slight forward bend
Shows respect for the Triple Gem.

The emptiness inside the hat
Symbolizes the changeless reality-body.
The black headband around the brow
Denotes the changeless enjoyment-body.
Hair waving in the wind signifies
The emanation-bodies streaming from the hat.
And the straps tied tightly at the back of neck
Represent the binding seal of mahamudra.

The thin waist of the damaru-drum
Marks the place of error and doubt
Where samsara and nirvana meet;
The widening out to the two skull-rims
Is like the waxing and waning of samsara and nirvana.

Skins stretched tight across both faces
Indicate explicit and implicit meanings,
The emptiness inside is like
The reality-body achieved for one's own sake.

The shell-adorned strap around the waist
Symbolizes the ornamented enjoyment-body;
The clappers striking against the skins are
The emanation-bodies streaming from it.
And the sound it makes when spun
Shows mastery over warriors and dakinis.

The hand-held strap
Indicates upholding the precepts for practice.
The banner tied to it
Is the fluttering banner of renown,
And the three-tiered banner head
Shows nonattachment to samsara's three realms.

The small, clear mirror in its center
Indicates life in the clear light;
Its symmetrical design
Signifies method and wisdom integrated.

Rows of ivory beads adorning it
Indicate unfailing memory.
Its pearl and coral decorations
Symbolize the seeds of auspicious bodily signs.

Silken tassels dangling down
Symbolize the five types of gnosis,
And the hanging lock of hair
Signifies work on behalf of those in samsara.

The tight, fine braid
Shows the three disciplines intertwining.
The small bells
Proclaim renown to the ten directions.
And the attached clasp
Shows adherence to the liberated life.

Do you get my meaning, ascetics?
Listen further, friends:
Without encountering a good lama,
Without instructions, precepts, and experience,
One is led by the appearances of this mundane life.

Though you have a yogin's form,
If you don't have good qualities of realization,

Wearing that white hat on your head
Is like whitewashing charcoal.

That white felt lining
Is like wrapping dog dung with fine wool,
And the white cotton covering
Is so much snow fallen on your head—
Gradually blackened with grime
By involvement with the filth of evil deeds.

Those long ear flaps on either side
Show that you'll wander in samsara a very long time.
That blue ribbon wound round the edge
Shows the ignorance which infects your mind.

That mirror fixed in front
Shows you abide in the depths of samsara;
And the long, high peak indicates
That you've scaled the peak of pride.

The five colored silk adornments
Signal the spread of five poisonous afflictions,
And the decorations of flowers
Mark your abundance of distractions and desire.

Those artificial braids
Are a sign of falling to lower states;
The slight forward bend is
A sign of great desire for food.

The emptiness inside the hat
Reflects the emptiness of human life.
That black headband worn round your brow,
Is like the great cloud-bank of delusion.

Your hair blowing in the wind
Shows you're agitated by the three poisons,[79]

189

And the straps tied tightly at the back of the neck
Show you're tightly bound to samsara.

The thin waist of the damaru-drum
Indicates your extreme paucity of wisdom;
Its widening out to the two skull rims
Shows how your sin and evil actions increase.

Skins stretched tight across both faces
Show you're veiled by the two obscurations.
The emptiness inside the drum
Shows the emptiness of this life and the next.

That shell-adorned strip around the waist
Is a true sign of a twisted mind.
The clappers striking against the skins
Mimic your knocking at doors for food.
And the sound the drum makes when spun
Proclaims the laughter of derision.

Its hand-held strap
Represents the mumbled songs caught in your throat.
The banner tied to it
Is your fluttering banner of disgrace,
And the three-tiered banner head
Reflects your wandering in samsara's three realms.

The small, clear mirror at its center
Reflects your actions,
And its symmetrical design
Is the laying of samsara's foundation.

The drum is adorned with rows of ivory beads
To show the succession of your sinful acts;
It's decorated with pearls and coral
To mock you wearing the ornaments of delusion.

The silken tassels dangling down
Show a mind streaming out through the five senses.
The hanging lock of hair indicates
Your plunge to lower states of life.

The tight, fine braid
Indicates the tightening of attachment to self.
The attached small bells
Broadcast your mumbled songs to the ten directions.
And that clasp-pin
Shows you're stuck in samsara's three realms.

Do you get my meaning, ascetics?
If you understand, it's dharma.
But listen again friends:

That was my song
About the three articles of ascetics—
Hat, headband, and damaru-drum—
Taking their details as examples.

It should be an iron goad
For yogins who have realization,
Provisions for those who wander the countryside,
Food for those seeking sustenance,
Nourishment for those in retreat,
A companion for those living alone,
And a standard for the masses.

You yogins who don't have realization,
Who wander the ends of the earth searching for food—
You will take the first set of examples
As the accomplice of imposters.
Use it to sate your rapacious hunger!
Use it as a crutch for lack of ability!
Hawk it as a treasure in the market!
Sing it as your song to the ten directions!

The second series of examples
Reveals the hidden nature of imposters.
The wise should take it as an admonition.
The unrealized should take it as derision.
Children should make it their nursery rhyme.
It should be repeated all day long.

Prompted by the situation,
I composed this allegory of appearances,
Making both good and bad examples;
Did you understand or not?

If you did, let it urge you to virtue.
If not, it will upset your mind.
Please be patient at my teasing.
I've considered all this, and my mind is happy.

View resting on the natural state is blissful.
Meditation lacking expectation is blissful.
Practice taking whatever comes is blissful.
Resultant lack of hope and fear is blissful.

Whatever I do is blissful.
I do it because it is blissful.
If you would have such joy,
Do this also.

Inspired with strong faith, they paid their respects, placed Mila's feet on their heads, and requested blessings and dharma teachings. After receiving instructions for meditation they practiced and gained unusual experience and realization. Later they became known as "The Four Yogins," and were renowned as especially high repas. This is the song called "Hat, Headband and Damaru-drum."

The Six Secret Songs

Jetsun Milarepa, lord of yogins, went to Mount Tisay with two disciples, defeated the Bön priest Naro Bonchung in a contest of miraculous powers, and thus established Tisay as a practice site for Buddhists.[80]

While staying in the Miracle Cave there Jetsun said to Rechungpa, "You have obtained the precepts of the Dakinis' Ear-whispered Tantras, thus completing the transmission of the instructional lineage.[81] To achieve results in this lifetime you must now put them into practice."

Rechungpa asked, "Please sing me a song expressing the keys for obtaining enlightenment in this lifetime."

Jetsun replied, "My ultimate precept is this." He turned around and exposed his buttocks—they were prominently covered with hard callouses from long periods of sitting meditation.[82]

On seeing this, Rechungpa was overwhelmed with admiration and respect for the austerities in practice endured by his lama. Tears welled up in his eyes and he thought with conviction, "I, too, must practice like this."

Milarepa then sang the Six Secret Songs:

Song of the Directionless Retreat

Father who is free from the bonds of egoism—
By achieving the goal where bliss and voidness are united,
The clear-light body of the two realities,
My father-lama dwells always in my heart.

While meditating on the neck of Tisay snow mountain,
I, Milarepa, clearly perceived the mandala of phenomena.
If you seek clairvoyance, I have obtained it;
I am a yogin aimed at the highest.

At the agate block of the Red Rock in Chu Bar
I flew in the sky without falling.
If you wish miraculous powers, I have obtained them;
I am a yogin aimed at the highest.

In the valley of Tsering white snow mountain
I was not panicked by the demons of the three realms.
If you wish the power to subdue demons, I have obtained it;
I am a yogin aimed at the highest.

While meditating on Lachi snow mountain
A host of dakinis gathered like a cloud.
If you wish siddhis, I have obtained them;
I am a yogin aimed at the highest.

This came from long meditation,
Let these scars on my ass
Impress upon you the import of this, my son;
Bear this great advice well in heart.
It is best to make practice your constant companion.

Song of the Mantra Path Entire

I pray at the feet of my reverend father—
Glorious, unshakable essence of vajra.

Though I am now Milarepa, I am certain
This body of leisure and opportunity will end;
This ravine of samsara is a vast abyss,
And I fear the narrow track of birth and death.

When I think that this wandering in samsara
Lasts till the forces of action and effect are stilled,
I know it is time to end this illusion of ego.

How could I bear the way these beings
Of the six realms, our kind mothers, are tormented by misery?

Thus, I sought the path for quickly achieving
This body of conquerors, leader of beings.

First, by conferral of the vase empowerment
My common body was identified with the deity's body.
By the secret empowerment of the current of speech,
Currents flowing in the right and left channels
Were drawn into the central channel.

By igniting the bliss of the third empowerment of wisdom
I saw the naked maiden of the egoless sphere.
By recognition of the four bodies symbolically expressed
In the fourth empowerment of words,
I came face to face with the unity of the three bodies.

After entering the initiatory doors, I practiced the two phases
And unified with space and awareness
The deity's body produced earlier on the path.

This unification of space and awareness is Vajradhara.
For this purpose the emanation-body of Shakyamuni appeared.
This is victory over birth, death, and bardo.

Having obtained the three bodies for myself,
I have no hope or fear about other results.
This came from long meditation,
As witnessed by these scars on my ass
Which I have kept secret from everyone but you.

These are my precepts to you, son Rechungpa,
The song of Mila Dorje Gyentsen.

Song of the Wish-granting Gem of Fulfillment

I bow to the feet of my holy father,
Consistently kind translator, best of men,
Who saw the unity of samsara and nirvana

And communicated his vision to others
With discriminating insight
Into good and bad, opportune and inopportune.

You must correctly keep and nurture
Your precious vows and commitments.
Your vajra-brothers, lama, personal deity,
Dakinis, guardians, protectors, and so on
Are the excellent benefits of keeping these commitments.

The holy lama is the embodiment of all buddhas,
His voice expresses the inexpressible,
His mind is the omnidirectional sunlight of method and
    wisdom.

One who realizes that all actions
Of a *true* lama's body, speech, and mind—
Farming, stealing, even killing—are virtuous.
Those who see them as a buddha's acts,
Are the best disciples for practicing the profound path.

Once mind is stamped with the seal of facing Tathagatas
By identification of your mind with heruka,
Dwelling place, food, clothes, and so on
Are experienced as spontaneous play.

Through the method and wisdom of my special lama
My vision toward friends and others was purified.
All these beings are my mothers—
Blind, crazed by afflictions—
Yogin, how can you bear it?
Dedicate yourself in service to beings.

Woman is essentially wisdom,
Source of spontaneous gnosis and illusory-body.
Never consider her inferior;
Strive especially to see her as Vajravarahi.

Enjoy common and special enjoyments
With the yogas of the six divine Conquerors.[83]

Never worship a deity with offerings of ordinary food and
    clothes
As common men worship a king.
When power objects are used in ordinary ways
It is like pouring clean milk into a dirty bucket.

The precept of nonseparation and preservation
Is the commitment to keep and never be without
Bone ornaments, vajra bell, and so on.

Maintain these fourteen major commitments,
And with them the eight subsidiaries.
Son and disciples who are vessels of dharma
Abandon all prohibited acts by observing these well.

It is a general precept that the Mantra Vehicle is secret,
And Peerless Tantra especially secret.
Personal deity Chakrasamvara is secret,
And the three seats—heart, intestine, and skull—are secret.

Vajravarahi is also secret
And the wish-granting gem of Ear-whispered Tantras.
Glorious space-like Guhyasamaja is secret,
And secret is the profound Hevajra Tantra.

Deity, mantra, and mudra are secret.
Empowerment, practice-time, and precepts are secret.
If you do not preserve these you will be burnt;
If preserved, you will achieve all siddhis.

Song of the Three Wish-granting Gems and the Six Yogas of Naropa

I pray to my holy father lamas,
Divine embodiments of voidness and great bliss,

My all-wise reverend lamas,
Whose minds are absorbed in the bliss-void state.

I have great faith in this lineage.
For one who has such faith,
The lineage of Tilopa, Naropa, and their successors
Is a wish-granting gem.

I, the yogin, have great faith in empowerment.
For one who has such faith,
There are three empowerments—
Developmental, liberative and fructifying—
And the six comprising the wealth of the developmental path.

I, the repa, have great faith in commitments.
For one who has faith in
The precious gems of inner and outer vows,
The mind is arranged in an instant.

In general, all appearances are divine manifestations,
And in particular, one's own being manifests as a deity
Through absorption in the state of heruka.
Thus, I have no fear of the narrow track of birth and death.

Rechungpa, I have given you the precepts
Which are the master key to the best of paths:
To tummo, illusory-body, dream, clear light,
Transference, and bardo.[84]
Take them to heart, son, do not repeat them.
I have sealed my lips to all but you.

Song of Tummo Yoga

I bow to the feet of the mantra holder,
Holy emanation-body of buddhas,
All-pervading sunshine of realization and experience
Who has cultivated of currents, channels, and drops.

In general, this practice is a secret shortcut.
In particular, the eye which sees Vajravarahi
Will later see three tummo stages: low, middle, high;
Tongue of flame, full of bliss, and so on,
As though from inside the sun.[85]

Knots of the right and left channels
Are freed into their natural state
By the Vajrasattva mantra which draws
The current in and out of the central channel.
Do not place trust in any mental support
Other than Vajrasattva mantra repetition.

Experience like a cloudless sky develops by
Binding the flow of life force
From the heart center to the central channel
With the yoga of coarse and fine currents.

Equalize the fluctuation of red and white elements
    in the navel center;
Realization and bliss-warmth experience then dawns
    in the mind.
Bear this in mind, son. Apply it in meditation.
This is transmitted only in succession.

Song of Illusory-body and Dream Yoga

I bow to the holy lamas and
Glorious, ever-present Lord Heruka,
Who cavorts in the realm of great bliss
Clasped round the neck by consort Vajravarahi.
Father Vajradhara, grant me blessings!

Son, you are the "Dorje Dragpa" foretold by dakinis;
If you think like this it is best.

In general, there are three types of illusions:

The confused illusion about appearances and voidness,
Visionary illusions of mind-created deity,
And hallucinatory illusions from abnormal currents and mind.

To understand the workings of these three
You must stop the flow in right and left channels.
Stopping in and out breath would be better.
Currents and mind are then absorbed in the clear light state.

You must also melt the white element
So that it drips into the central channel.
Thus, by the power of blazing, immaculate bliss
The ten major currents
And 21,600 minor currents
Arise from the circular hollow of the central channel.

In particular, deities and their unmeasured mansions
Arise from subtle, supple currents and mind
And are revealed in attendance on the lama's enjoyment body.

In the state between sleep and dream,
In the palace where in- and out-breath stop,
The experience of great bliss clear-light manifests
Through meditationless gnosis.

When the imprintings for illusory dreams are activated
You must realize the nature of appearance and voidness
Through recognition of the illusion of dream
In the birthless void state
And create your own dream emanations of void appearances.

You must practice the precepts for the three transformations:
The general transformation of the apparent world into the
    divine,
The particular manifestation of deity's body in dream
Through manipulation of mind and currents,
And the emanation of bodies, clairvoyance, and so on.

Take this as my song of practice,
A secret discourse fallen from my lips.
It's only the laughter of a very happy old man.

Son, Rechungpa, it is my act of mercy;
I've manifested the rainbow-body in this life.

This is my transmission for practice,
The song of Mila Dorje Gyentsen.

Song of
Impermanence

After Milarepa had departed from Pelmo Plateau, he encountered a patron who asked him, "Yogin, please sing a melodious song that penetrates to the heart of things." So Mila sang:

I bow to the feet of Translator Marpa,
Emanation-body of universal ruler,
Face of all Buddhas—past, present, and future—
Indistinguishable from Vajradhara.
I pray to you with more than words,
Bless me from the depths of space.

Eh ma! Fortunate ones gathered here,
Though I cannot compose melodious songs,
I will teach you about impermanence.
Hear me with undistracted minds.

At the end of life we will surely die,
The flow of breath will certainly stop,
The vulture of mind will inevitably fly off.
Now, while we have the chance,
We must first practice our whole lives,
Next, abandon the ten evil deeds,
And last, pray day and night.

What has been gathered will separate,
Mind and body will surely part,

Limbs and joints will disintegrate.
So first, we must eliminate interest in this life,
Next, leave our homeland far behind,
And last, practice all year round.

What has been acquired will vanish,
Hoarded possessions will inevitably be lost,
And prosperity will eventually decline.
So first, we must do our best,
Next, be satisfied with what we have,
And last, practice impartial giving.

Today I am Mila, tomorrow a corpse;
In the morning a rich man, by evening a pauper;
Now as a single entity, in an instant scattered—
The inevitable outcome for all composed things.

Like the streaming river Tsangpo
Nothing is still for even a moment.
Like the twilight between day and night,
Life will also swiftly fade.

Consider this, and practice dharma.
Consider this, and practice giving.

The patron was deeply impressed and made many offerings.

Mila's Final Teachings

After singing two thousand songs for humans and gods, the great Jetsun Milarepa was staying at Chu Bar, practicing with his close disciples. He told them, "Nowadays there are those who appear to be good practitioners of religion; they appear to have merit. But they only apply themselves in this life with ambitious intentions, engaging in charity with the strategy of sacrificing a hundred important or unimportant things to gain a thousand in return. Although it displeases wise men, these worldly people persist with such duplicity.

"Many others are industrious in pursuing virtue, anxious about the fading lustre of this life, but they have not renounced their concern for fame. This is like eating good food after mixing it with poison. Therefore, refrain from drinking the poisoned water of desire for fame in this life. Renounce concern for all affairs aimed at fulfilling mundane ambitions. Strive to practice virtue.

"Beings will endure until the sky itself vanishes. If you have the will to practice, there will come a time for benefitting beings. Until then, be humble in your practice and firmly resolve to attain Buddhahood for the sake of all beings, valuing them above yourself.

"Clothe yourself in rags. Take up practice, enduring the physical hardships and mental burdens of disregard for food, clothes, and recognition. *That* is the welfare of beings. Furthermore, to set your practice off on the right track, all this should be remembered." And Mila sang this song:

I bow to the feet of Translator Marpa.

Dharma followers who wish to practice:
For one who does not serve a qualified lama,
Aspiration and devotion yield small results.

For one lacking profound empowerment,
Tantra brings entanglement in words.

For one who does not take the tantras as his standard,
All practice is a cause of hindrance.

For one who fails to meditate on the profound precepts,
Denial of worldly life is self-torture.

The speech of one who has not cured affliction with antidote[86]
Is nothing but sound, empty and dry.

For one who is ignorant of the profound path of method,
Diligence will be short on results.

For one lacking a deep sense of what to do and not do,
The path will be long in spite of much effort.

For one who has not applied much effort,
Singular self-interest is the cause of samsara.

For one who has not applied merit to practice,
Meditation will fail to produce realization.

For one who has not found contentment within,
Hoarded possessions only enrich others.

For one who lacks inner bliss,
External pleasures are a cause of pain.

For one who has not conquered the devil of ambition,
Desire for fame brings self-destruction and discord.

Striving for pleasure stirs the five poisonous afflictions.
Striving for wealth estranges fond friends.
Striving for fame brings much contention.

Keep your mouth shut and there will be no quarrels.
Cultivate nondistractedness and distractions cease.
Live alone and you will find a friend.
Take the low place and you will reach the highest.
Practice slowly and you will soon arrive.
Renounce worldly affairs and you will reach the goal.
Travel the arduous path and you will find the shortcut.

When you realize voidness, compassion will arise.
When compassion arises, partiality will vanish.
When partiality is gone, beings' welfare is accomplished.
When beings' welfare is accomplished, you will meet with me.
And by meeting me, Buddhahood is achieved.

Pray to me, the Buddha, and my disciples,
Not discriminating one from the others.

Then Jetsun continued, "I do not know how long I will stay now. Having listened to me, you should do as I have done. Follow me . . . follow me. . . ."

Then, after entering a state of equanimity, the great Jetsun absorbed his physical body into the reality-realm at the age of eighty-four years, at dawn of the fourteenth day of the last winter month (February) during the female wood-hare year (1136 AD) at the rising of the constellation Ashlesha.

Meanwhile, Rechungpa was staying at the monastery of Loro Dol. In the later part of the night, while experiencing a state of sleep and clear light combined, two women appeared in the sky. They said, "If you do not go quickly to meet your lama, he will go to the celestial realm of the dakinis and you will not meet him again in this lifetime."

Thinking, "I must go at once," Rechungpa rose and left as the cocks of Loro Dol were beginning to crow. In a state of intensely fervent guru-yoga, Rechungpa controlled his breath and went forth to meet his lama at the speed of an arrow, covering in one morning the distance it would take two months to travel by donkey. He reached the top of Bosay Pass between Ding Ri and Drin as the first sunbeams lit the mountain peaks. There he rested briefly. The sky and air, the mountaintops, and all the earth were filled with auspicious signs, bringing him both joy and sadness. He pressed on quickly.

On the road near Chu Bar, on top of the large boulder shaped like the base of a stupa, he met Mila. The Jetsun said to him with pleasure, "Have you come, my son Rechungpa?"

Thinking, "It's not true that Jetsun is dying," Rechungpa was filled with immeasurable joy and placed Jetsun's feet on his head.

Jetsun answered all of Rechungpa's questions, and then said, "Son, Rechungpa, I am going on to prepare a reception for you. Come a little later." He went on ahead, and in a moment disappeared from sight.

Rechungpa continued traveling. Arriving at Chu Bar, he found everyone—monks, close disciples, and laymen—gathered at Jetsun's usual dwelling cave, worshipping his corpse in the numbness of grief. Filled with an intense sorrow, Rechungpa approached the funeral pyre, which had previously refused to kindle, and offered this lament to his lama:

Precious buddha of the three times, refuge of beings,
From the depths of your wisdom and love
Do you hear the anguished mourning
Of your poor disciple, Rechungpa Dorje Drak?

This lament burst out uncontrollably, precious lama.
Wanting to join you, I came to your feet,
But this unworthy son failed to see your face.
Father, watch after me with compassion, have mercy.

At Rechungpa's sincere lament, Mila arose from his absorption in the clear light and said, "Do not choke on your grief, Rechungpa. Come to your father."

Everyone was amazed. Rechungpa took hold of Jetsun and wept profusely and then he fainted. When he revived he found all the monks and disciples standing in a line before the blazing pyre. Jetsun had risen again in the indestructible vajra-body, pressing down the flames with his hands into the shape of an eight-petaled lotus and sitting in the center with legs half-crossed, like the pistil of a flower. Pressing down the flames with his right hand extended in a teaching gesture, Jetsun put his left hand to the side of his head and said, "Disciples, children, I will answer Rechungpa. Listen to the last words of this old man." And from the throat of his vajra-body within the pyre arose this final Song of the Six Essential Keys:

Son like my own heart, Rechungpa,
Hear this song—my last testament.

In the three realms of samsara's ocean
This illusory body is the great culprit.
Obsessed with cravings for food and clothes,
There's no time to give up worldly works.
Renounce mundane affairs, Rechungpa.

In the city of the illusory body
The unreal mind is the great culprit.
Obsessed with the body of flesh and blood,
There's no time to realize reality's import.
Control this mundane mind, Rechungpa.

On the border between body and mind
The conditioned intellect is the great culprit.
Changing with the flux of ephemeral conditions,
There's no time to realize the unborn meaning.
Keep to the stronghold of the unborn, Rechungpa.

At the boundary of this life and the next
The bardo consciousness is the great culprit.
Disembodied, always seeking a form,
There's no time to realize the natural state.
Ascertain the natural state, Rechungpa.

In the city of the six illusory realms
Evil action is the great hindrance,
Following the dictates of likes and dislikes,
There's no chance to realize impartiality.
Abandon partiality, Rechungpa.

Somewhere in the unmanifest realm of space
The perfect buddha is a liar.
Speaking deceptively of implicit meanings,
There's no chance to realize the explicit truth.
Abandon conventional facts, Rechungpa.

Lama, personal deity, and dakinis,
Pray to these three rolled into one.

View, meditation, and action,
Practice these three rolled into one.

This life, the next, and the bardo state,
Acquaint yourself with these three rolled into one.

These are the last of all my precepts,
And of my final testament the end;
Than this, there is no other truth, Rechungpa.
Apply this in practice, oh my son.

Mila absorbed himself into the clear light again, and immediately afterwards rainbow light suffused the pyre and took on the shape of a vast square mansion with four ornate entryways. Upon it there appeared rainbow tents and canopies, parasols, and banners adorning its cornices, and innumerable offerings filling the interior. The bases of the flames retained the shape of an eight-petaled lotus, while their tips flickered into the forms of the eight auspicious symbols and various offerings such as the seven precious things. All sparks shot out in the form of goddesses holding offerings and worshipping, and all the sounds of burning became the sweet sounds of music—strings, reeds, brass, and drums. Even the smoke was sweet-smelling and condensed into rainbow-colored clouds shaped like various offerings—parasols, banners, and so on. All the while, gods and goddesses bearing vessels appeared in the sky above the funeral pyre and satisfied all present with a rainfall of nectar and pleasures for the five senses.

Epilogue

Advice to Young Dampa Gyakpuba

Once while staying at Tsarma of Nya Nang, Mila was teaching dharma to some disciples at the foot of a tree. The famous Dampa Gyakpuba, then a young novice, was among them.[87] Jetsun stroked his head with his hand and said, "Son, listen to this song of advice."

Homage to the feet of my holy lama.

Some of the monks ordained
Into Conqueror Muni's doctrine
Wear religious robes outside
While inside are still attached to this life.

They abstain from beer and afternoon food,
But hoard wealth like laymen;
Wash their mouths out after eating,
But utter nonsense, lies and slander.

Outwardly, they act with wise discretion,
But are driven by three poisons within.
Son, do not accompany such friends.

Some meditators in this degenerate age
Consider tranquilization experience supreme.

They believe mere bliss and clarity final,
Not realizing the goal, the natural state.

Some recite fruitless ritual,
Sight set only on food and money.
With partiality and prejudice surpassed by none,
They teach dharma randomly, like a hobby.

They act with guile before other's wealth,
Their own wealth kept selfishly ungiven.
Great acquisition, little patience.
Son, do not accompany such friends.

Mantra practitioners in this evil time
Grow their hair into long matted tresses
And tie shaman's beads around their neck
Without developing the stages of production and completion.

Though channels and element[88] are naturally divine
And their life-force must be preserved from danger,
False monks sleep with women just like laymen.
They give the title "ritual feast"
To their excuses for consuming meat and beer.
Son, do not accompany such friends.

"Especially to you, son, a share of dharma will come, but you must attend this old man. For controlling your own mind there is no better dharma than what I am about to tell you; therefore, strive to practice it.

"You should realize the natural state through mental control, then meditate one-pointedly until realization develops. The goal of unmistaken reality is realized by such meditation and its associated experiences. There is no better dharma for cultivating ultimate realization.

"Until the goal of reality's natural state is reached, any purification of obscurations will be infected by one of the eight worldly concerns of this life. Therefore, strive to control your mind.

"Listen carefully now to this old man. *When you have grown older you will not be able to sit under this tree which today casts a cool shadow on us, teacher and disciples*. Son, it is said that religious projects are the ground for cultivating the roots of virtue. But if they are poisoned by any of the eight worldly concerns it would be better to build a temple of the mind. *Do not kill insects by disrupting isolated places.*" Mila then sang this song:

Homage to Lama Vajradhara.

This illusory body built of four elements
On the elemental foundation of food, breath, and the like,
Is an immeasurable mansion with four walls.

On lotus and sun in the heart of this mansion,
(One's body composed of the elements and the others)
Ornamented with four doors, thresholds, senses,
Jeweled vajra nets, half-nets, and so on,
Build the divine mandala of appearance-void union
For the deity of groups, elements, and media.[89]

Offer constant worship—inner, outer, and secret.
Attain the completion-stage state of bliss-void gnosis.
Without good cause, leave wild animals be.

At a much later time, after Dampa Gyakpuba had become a famous teacher, while building a temple at Tsarma he cut down that very same tree. When he saw that he had destroyed many ant-hills while excavating the foundation, he suddenly remembered Jetsun's words and was stunned. He then knew that Milarepa was truly an omniscient buddha. To repay his kindness, he made renewed efforts in practice.

Notes

1. These are the twelve linked causal factors (*nidāna*) leading to existence in samsara. The others are the six sense faculties, sense contact, feeling, craving, attachment, existence, birth, old age and death.
2. Wherein the being is repeatedly slain and revived. This verse expresses the bodhisattva's willingness to enter hell if necessary to aid beings.
3. Vows of "temporary abstinence" (*upavasa*) from killing, stealing, lying, improper sexual activity, and fasting.
4. The aspiration to help others attain liberation and the implementation of this intent in one's behavior.
5. Of body, speech, and mind.
6. Corresponding to the five meditation Buddhas (see "Five Meditation Buddhas" in the glossary).
7. Padmasambhava's meditation cave in western Bhutan.
8. Literally "action gesture" (*karma mudrā*), which indicates the practice of sexual intercourse with a human partner.
9. In the following song Mila addresses him as Ja Tön—"Teacher of Ja."
10. Scholar-meditators (*geshés*) whose system of practice was based on careful analysis of original Indian Buddhist sources.
11. Habitual conceptualization or insistence (*abhiniveśa*) means automatic conceptualization of personal and phenomenal identities with regard to composed things which are merely the products of causal elements.
12. Expectations, fears, success, failure, wealth, poverty, praise, and censure.
13. "Vows for personal liberation" (*pratimokṣa*) are those for monks and nuns of the Lesser Vehicle. There is no actual mental evil in the Lesser Vehicle. Mental action serves only as the motivation for physical and verbal evils. In general evils are of two types: those specifically prohibited by one's vows and those which are naturally evil.
14. This includes the cultivation of the absorption (*dhyāna*) levels and generation

of the mind aimed at enlightenment. It is universally directed because it is aimed at the liberation of all beings, not just one's self.

15. This refers to the eight-process model of mind of the Yogācārya system: the five sensory processes, the conscious process, the dualistic afflictive mentality, and the basis or fundamental (*ālaya*) process which patterns all present experience through traces resulting from past experience.

16. Homage, offering, confession, rejoicing in others' spirituality, turning the wheel of the dharma, requesting Buddhas not to pass into nirvana, and dedication of merit of your own practice.

17. The two stores or accumulations of personal power: merit, the accumulated effects of behavioral control and correct deeds; and gnosis, which here applies to any correct knowledge. These stores are compiled on the accumulation path, prior to the first experience of transcendence. For a detailed explanation of the hundred-syllable mantra, mandala, and other practices see *The Torch of Certainty* and *Tantric Practice in Nyingma* (see references, p. 232).

18. Refers to *guruyoga*.

19. Moral behavior, tranquilization meditation and cultivation of analytic insight.

20. See glossary under individual terms.

21. Excitation is over-arousal causing distractibility of the attention from its object. Depression is under-arousal causing an unfocused sinking into the object and eventually sleep. Discursiveness means the habitual leap of the mind to identify and name its object.

22. *Prajñāpāramitā* and *pramāṇa*.

23. Mila is using the technical terminology of formal buddhist epistemology (*pramāna*).

24. *gZha.gdong.dmar.nag.* The spells mentioned here belong to the prebuddhist shamanistic cult of Tibet.

25. Rong.ston.lha.ga' was a lama of the Nyingma sect. The "Great Perfection" (*rdzogs.pa.chen.po*) is a system of practice roughly similar to the *mahāmudrā* of the Kagyupa lineage.

26. The *Ḍākinī-karṇa-tantras*; the one named is *Lhan.cig.skyad.sbyor*.

27. The four strengths for purifying sins are: faith, self-censure or regret, renewed commitment to act correctly, and maintenance of antidotes of evil behavior.

28. The seven classes of this *pratimokṣa* commitment include the orders of men and women devotees (*upāsika*), novices (*śrāmanera*), and monks and nuns (*bhikṣu/bhikṣuṇī*). The four main breaches which apply to all seven classes are killing, stealing, lying, and sexual misconduct.

29. *Triskandha-sūtra*.

30. "Entrance" to the initiatory mandala drawn with colored sand on the ground.
31. The fourteen lapses of tantric commitments are from the *Kṛṣṇayamāri-tantra*:

Do not despise your teacher.
Do not stray from the Sugata's Teaching.
Do not criticize or feel anger
Toward your brothers.
Do not give up the bodhi-mind.
Do not despise your own or other's religion.
Show pure loving-kindness toward all living beings,
Never abandoning them.
Do not show secret teachings
To beings who are not completely ripened.
Do not abuse the aggregates of yourself or others.
Do not trouble the existence of worldly people.

Always give love, even to the worst.
Do not discriminate between the teachings.
Do not deceive the faithful.
Always keep your vows.
It is also wrong to despise
The wisdom nature of women.
Do not feel that yogis are beggars,
And always respect them.

Always repeat the secret mantras,
And always keep your vows.
Yet, if through carelessness
You should break your vow to the Lama,
Draw the sacred mandala
And confess your failure before the Sugatas.
Without doubt, with compassion,
And with faithful mind, guard your vow to the Lama.

32. That is, through the four centers (*cakra*)—the navel, heart, throat, and head.
33. Co-disciples of the same tantric teacher.
34. Short lifespan, perverse views, abundance of mental afflictions, undisciplined beings and obstructive conditions.
35. The keys to understanding and practice provided in scriptures are of two kinds: those of explicit content which succinctly state their meaning, and those of implicit content which must be interpreted before application in practice.

36. Integration of method and wisdom.
37. This refers to the custom of returning the last portion of a food offering to the giver (*prasād*).
38. The superficial and absolute levels of reality.
39. The path of method, which is the complement of the "path of liberation," includes generation of the mind aimed at enlightenment, the four tantric preparatory practices, personal-deity yoga, the perfecting yogas (dream, clear-light, transference, and so on), manipulation of the subtle current-mind complex, and so forth.
40. *Vinaya, Abhidharma,* and *Pāramitā.*
41. The Goddess Tseringma, Mila's personal consort. See stories in *The Hundred-thousand Songs of Milarepa* (hereafter, simply *100,000 Songs*), in chapters 28, 29, and 31.
42. Compare this song to the first song in chapter 59 of *100,000 Songs.*
43. See glossary: evils, ten.
44. "Vows of purification" (*poṣadha*) are closely associated with the keeping of temporary abstinence (*upavasa*) on the significant full moon, new moon, and eighth days of each month.
45. That is, eliminate concepts of ego and identity from the three conceptual spheres of agent-action, the object involved, and the recipient or goal of the action.
46. sNeu.zur.pa (1042–1118), a famous Kadampa lama-scholar (*geshé*) of Lhasa who had over one thousand disciples. See *The Blue Annals*, pages 111–114, translated by George N. Roerich, Delhi: Motilal Banarsidass, 1976.
47. *Avatāra-bodhicitta.* Actions motivated by the aspiration that all beings attain enlightenment.
48. sPyan.nga.pa (the Presence), another famous Kadampa geshé.
49. From here to the end of the second song the story parallels a fragment contained in the *100,000 Songs*, chapter 60, describing Mila's interaction with "A Tantric Yogi of Ü."
50. Spirit traps are geometric devices of sticks and string, something like a Native American god's eye but in three dimensions, which serve as maze-like traps for harmful spirits.
51. Ordinary siddhis (accomplishments) are powers on the superficial level, such as flying, clairvoyance, and so on. The supreme siddhi is enlightenment.
52. That is, the Kagyupa lineage.
53. This refers to the removal of obstructive conditions, all of which, whether internal or external, originate in the mind. The "weapon" in this line turns or spins, and is perhaps synonymous with the "wheel weapon" of certain "mind purification" teachings (*blo.byong*), where it symbolizes the mind's destruction

of its own egocentric tendencies through the force of these tendencies themselves.

54. Nada-sound refers to the inherent, residual "hum" of the apparent world, which merges with voidness at its most refined limit.

55. The four propositions are *to exist, not exist, exist and not exist* (simultaneously), and *neither exist nor not exist*—all the ways of perceiving the identities of persons and things.

56. From the *Mūla-mādhyamika-kārika* of Ārya Nāgārjuna.

57. Lama Kunga and Brian Cutillo, *Drinking the Mountain Stream*, New York: Lotsawa, Inc., 1978, pages 92 et seq.

58. The three commitments are personal liberation (*pratimokṣa*), the bodhisattva's vow, and the Tantric commitment. See the explanation of the three commitments in "Mila Teaches Two Scholars How to Practice" in Part Two.

59. Mt. Tisay has been identified as the triple-peaked Mt. Kailash, which has long been a sacred and popular pilgrimage spot for Buddhists of Tibet, Hindus, and Bönpos. The four rivers are the modern Sutlej, flowing west from Elephant-head Rock; the Brahmaputra, flowing east from Horse-head Rock; the Indus, flowing north from Tiger-head Rock; and the Irawaddy, flowing south from Owl-head Rock.

60. Soul-ransoming (*bla.bslu*) is an ancient, prebuddhist practice found throughout Tibet. See Tucci, *The Religions of Tibet*, Berkeley: UC Press, 1980, p 190 ff.

61. That is, empowerment to transfer the boy's consciousness to a better rebirth immediately upon death, without passing through the bardo state.

62. Uṣṇīṣavijayā represents long life; Kurukullā is a wrathful form of love.

63. See glossary: social means, four.

64. See glossary: torma.

65. See glossary for terms in this and the following verse.

66. The *upavasa* and *poṣadha* rituals.

67. The mythical founder of the Bön religion; see *Drinking the Mountain Stream*, "Confrontation with a Bön Priest," page 141.

68. For further discussion, see Evans-Wentz, *The Tibetan Book of the Dead*, pp. 6–8.

69. Refers to the practice of holding pebbles in the mouth to allay hunger during long periods of meditation.

70. One of the five meditation buddhas (see glossary).

71. Mila's earlier initiatory name.

72. Darbum believes that her dream foretells Mila's imminent death and departure from this world to take his place as Lord of Ḍākinīs.

73. This refers to the practice of dream yoga, one of the "Six Yogas of Naropa;" see glossary and "Six Secret Songs" (Part Five).

74. Devaputramāra, one of the "four devils," symbolizing compulsive belief in the validity of one's mental events.

75. The *ālaya-vijñāna*.

76. Bal.po.rdzong, perhaps in Kye Rong.

77. The saturative concentrations are a classic yogic method for gaining control of perceptual processes. The meditator produces a visualization of one of the four elements or primary colors strong enough to overlay or "saturate" usual perceptions of objects.

78. In this passage "element" refers to the "white element" or "drops" (*bindu*), which are ritually identified as semen. This is "melted" in the head center, and dripped down through four centers, yielding the four ecstasies. "Gnosis-consort" (*jñānamudrā*) is a mental consort consisting of gnosis, while "action-consort" (*karmamudrā*) is a human consort in tantric practice.

79. The three major negative mental functions, or "poisons" are ignorance, attachment and aversion.

80. This story is recounted in the *100,000 Songs*, chapter 22, "Miracle Contest at Tisay Snow Mountain."

81. The Ḍākinī-karṇa-tantras; see the *100,000 Songs*, chapter 35, "Rechungpa's Third Journey to India," and chapter 39, "Rechungpa's Repentance."

82. This "ultimate precept" was also given to Gampopa (see the *100,000 Songs*, chapter 41).

83. These are the yogas associated with the six meditation buddhas. In the Kagyupa mandala, Vajrasattva occupies the central position, while the figures at the four compass points are the same as in the other tantric lineages. The sixth is Vajradhara, who encompasses the integration of the other five.

84. These are the famous Six Yogas of Naropa (see Evans-Wentz, *Tibetan Yoga and Secret Doctrines*, London: Oxford University Press, 1935).

85. During the first phase of tummo yoga, the yoga of external heat, Vajravārāhī, the "Diamond Sow," is visualized. The subsequent lines deal with the phase of inner heat, from a small flame in the navel center to a larger flame extending to the heart center, then to the throat center, and finally consuming the whole environment.

86. "Antidote" refers specifically to the mental states or processes by which the negative emotional and cognitive states, called *afflictions*, are displaced or suppressed.

87. "Famous" refers to Dampa Gyakpuba's later life, when he was renowned as a builder of monasteries and founder of religious centers.

88. "Element" signifies white bindu, or drops.
89. "Groups" refers to the five groups (*skandha*) of psycho-physical constituents of a living being. Elements and media refer to the faculties of sensation and cognition.

Glossary

ABSORPTION, ABSORPTION LEVELS (*dhyāna*) The distinct, metastable states of mental operation attained through tranquilization of mental functioning by one-pointed concentration. Attainment of the eight successively more quiescent absorption levels—the first four comprising the form realm and the second four the formless realm—involves the suppression of thought and disturbing mental functions. The duration of each level depends on the force of the process of suppression. They are states common to all yoga and are entirely samsaric in nature.

ACTION (*karma*) Exactly that: any intentional or unintentional action performed through the "three doors": body, speech, and mind. There are three types: virtuous, yielding positive results; evil, yielding negative results; and fixed, which refers to action in a state of absorption which yields results that are "fixed" or limited to the absorption levels.

ACTION CONSORT *see* Karmamudrā.

AFFLICTIONS (*kleśa*) Negative mental functions and emotions which obstruct development. There are six primary afflictions: ignorance, desire, aversion, doubt, pride, and wrong views; and a number of subsidiary afflictions associated with their occurrence.

AKANIṢṬHA HEAVEN Abode of a bodhisattva just prior to birth in the world where he is to achieve final buddhahood.

AMITĀBHA One of the five Meditation Buddhas (*see* Five Meditation Buddhas).

ANALYTIC INSIGHT (*vipaśyanā*) The process of detailed examination of the meditation object as to its actual mode of existence. It involves thought and is aimed at penetrating the conceptual process. It results in tolerance to the direct perception of voidness.

ANALYTIC MEDITATION (*dpyod.sgom*) Meditational processes are either analytic (introspection of mind and its functioning) or focusing (the suppression of conceptual processes, as in concentration—the one-pointed focusing of attention on a single object to the exclusion of all others). To be effective, analytic techniques should be preceded by and conjoined with skill in concentration.

APPEARANCE, APPARENT WORLD (*snang.ba*)   Reality as it appears to a common individual whose conditioned, distorted perception experiences reality in the form of discrete, independent identities. Synonym: illusory world, superficial reality.

ARHAT   A person who has attained the final goal of the Lesser Vehicle, nirvana, the extinction of personal misery and elimination of rebirth.

ATTENTION (*manasikāra*)   Mental process which controls the direction and span of the consciousness.

AVALOKITESHVARA (Avalokita)   The bodhisattva who embodies compassion.

BARDO   The state of consciousness between death and rebirth.

BASIS PROCESS (*ālaya-vijñāna*)   *see* Fundamental Consciousness.

BODHISATTVA   Literally "Enlightenment Warrior;" dedicated to spiritual advancement and liberation in order to help others in their own development. To become a bodhisattva a person must generate the mind-for-enlightenment, or great compassion, and have some experience of the inherent voidness of self and world.

BÖN   The native religion of Tibet. Its followers are called Bönpo.

CHAKRASAMVARA   (*Chakrasamvara*) A personal deity (*yi.dam*) who embodies supreme happiness.

CENTERS (*cakra*)   The foci of the flow of current (*prana*) in the psycho-physiological system of tantric yoga. They are located at the head, throat, heart, and navel.

CHANNELS (*nadi*)   Pathways along which the currents (*prana*) move. The main channels are the central channel (*avadhuti*), and the right and left channels (*ida and pingala*).

CIRCLE FEAST (*tshogs.'khor*)   A feast of offering attended by the host of ḍākinīs.

CLEAR-LIGHT (*ābhāsvara, 'od.gsal*)   The experience of the natural, primal, unmodified state of the mind.

COGNITIVE PATTERNING   *see* Patterning.

COMPLETION PHASE   *see* Two Phases.

COMPULSIVE (*upadāna*)   Automatic, habitual—in reference to the patterning of mental functioning—involving perceptions, thought, and emotional reactions, according to the conditionings of past experience.

CONCENTRATION (*samādhi*)   The technique of controlling the mechanisms of attention through the focusing of attention on a single object. It is a development of the inherent capacity to "pay attention" and is a basic prerequisite for all advanced practices, such as analytic or introspective techniques.

CONDITIONING   *see* Compulsive.

CONQUEROR   A term for enlightened buddhas who have conquered the two obscurations.

CURRENTS (*prana*)   The psycho-physical forces of the mind, body, and environment.

ḌĀKA   Male counterpart of the ḍākinīs.

ḌĀKINĪ   Female tantric deities who aid the yogin and oversee his practice and behavior.

DEDICATION (*pariṇāma*)   Sharing one's virtuous actions, successful practice, and attainment with others. It consists of prayer, visualization, and attitude which should close each practice session, and also includes the dedication customarily given by yogis in return for food.

DEITY   *see* Personal Deity.

DEPENDENT OCCURRENCE (*pratītya-samutpāda*)   The twelve linked causal factors involved in the cycle of samsaric existence. In basic Buddhism, it refers to the succession and circumstances of rebirths, and in later thought is applied also to the production of each cognition of any phenomenal thing.

DHARMA-BODY (*dharma-kāya*)   *see* Three Bodies.

DHARMA-ELEMENT, DHARMA-REALM (*dharmadhātu*)   The ultimate reality of all things.

DISCIPLE (*śrāvaka*)   The disciples of Buddha Śākyamuni and the followers of their schools. There were eighteen such schools in India whose teachings comprise the Small Vehicle. In the specific sense it refers to persons who have attained arhatship.

DROPS (*bindu*)   "Substances" of the yogic psycho-physical system. In tantra the white bindu, or white element, is equivalent to the mind-for-enlightenment. It must be "melted" at the head center and "dripped" down the central channel to the lower centers, producing the four ecstasies.

EGO (*ātman*)   The imagined self or identity of persons (personal ego) and things (phenomenal ego) that are inherently lacking any independent identity.

EIGHT WORLDLY CONCERNS   Attitudes which inhibit spiritual development, consisting of the attraction and avoidance of pleasure and discomfort, praise and criticism, gain and loss, and status and loss of status.

EIGHTFOLD NOBLE PATH   The eight basic types of practice which lead to enlightenment: right view, right thought, right speech, right behavior, right livelihood, right effort, right mindfulness, and right meditation.

ELEMENT   *see* Drops.

EMANATION-BODY (*nirmāṇa-kāya*)   *see* Three Bodies.

EMPOWERMENT (*abhiṣeka*) Conferral of the inspiration and instructions for a practice; in particular, the four major tantric empowerments—called the *vase* or *pot*, the *secret*, *wisdom*, and *word*—which are directed toward development of body, speech, mind, and insight into ultimate reality, respectively.

ENJOYMENT-BODY (*saṁbhoga-kāya*) *see* Three Bodies.

ENLIGHTENMENT (*bodhi*) The state of buddhahood constituted by perfection of the two stores and removal of the two obscurations. It is the only level of attainment beyond the range of samsara.

ENLIGHTENMENT-MIND *see* Mind-for-Enlightenment.

ESSENTIAL-BODY (*svabhāva-kāya*) *see* Three Bodies.

EXCITATION AND DEPRESSION (*rgod.pa* and *bying.ba*) Refers to the spectrums of mental activation (autonomic arousal of the central nervous system). Excitation and depression lie on opposite sides of the optimal level of arousal for meditation practice, having adverse effects on the ability to focus attention in one-pointed concentration.

FABRICATION (*prapañca*) The internal stream of conceptualization directed by imprinted preconceptions. The term includes both the internal flow of thought-constructs and the self and environment they "create."

FIVE GNOSES (*jñāna*) *see* Five Meditation Buddhas.

FIVE MEDITATION BUDDHAS (*dhyāni-buddha*) Vairocana, the embodiment of dharma-realm wisdom, Akṣobhya, the embodiment of mirror-like wisdom, Ratnasambhava, the embodiment of equalizing wisdom, Amitābha, the embodiment of discriminating wisdom, and Amoghasiddhi, the embodiment of all-accomplishing wisdom.

FIVE POWERS (*pañcedriya*) Faith, effort, mindfulness, concentration, and wisdom.

FIVE STRENGTHS (*pañcabala*) *see* Five Powers.

FOCUSING MEDITATION (*'jog.sgom*) Meditation practices are either analytic (involving conceptual processes) or focusing, which involved one-pointed concentration on an object.

FOOD OF ABSORPTION, FOOD OF CONCENTRATION Nourishment during meditative states derived from concentrative absorption. It can sustain the yogin in place of food for periods of time.

FORM BODY (*rūpakāya*) Term for the enjoyment and emanation-bodies together (*see* Three Bodies).

FOUR BASES OF SUPERNORMAL POWERS (*ṛddhipāda*) Willingness, effort, attentiveness, and investigation.

FOUR DEVILS (*māra*)   Samsaric enemies to liberation; they are one's psycho-physical constituents, afflictive mental states, death, and external obstructions.

FOUR ELEMENTS (*dhātu*)   Earth (solidity), water (fluidity), fire (heat), and air (motility). Space is sometimes counted as a fifth element.

FOUR INFINITUDES (*apramāna*)   Basic emotions which can be developed into catalysts for generating the mind aimed at enlightenment (*bodhicitta*). They are love, compassion, joy, and mental equanimity.

FOUR SOCIAL MEANS (*samgrāha-vastu*)   Four practices performed by a bodhisattva primarily for others' welfare: giving, relevant communication, assisting the development of others, and serving as an example to others.

FRUSTRATED SPIRITS (*preta*)   *see* Six States.

FUNDAMENTAL CONSCIOUSNESS (*ālaya-vijñāna*)   The eighth consciousness, according to the Mind-only system developed by Asaṅga in the fifth century. It is the basic substratum of the individual's consciousness which carries the imprintings of "seeds" of past and future experience.

GESHÉ (*kalyāna-mitra*)   "Spiritual friend;" a title given to a person who has demonstrated exceptional competence in the scriptures and subjects of basic Buddhism.

GNOSIS (*jñāna*)   Generally, knowledge; specifically, the wisdom by which the apparent world and its reality are simultaneously perceived.

GREAT VEHICLE (*mahāyāna*)   *see* Vehicle.

HEROINE (*dba'.mo*)   Female counterpart of the tantric warrior (*dba'.wo*).

HERUKA   Wrathful aspect of a personal deity.

HIGHER STATES (*sugati*)   *see* Six States.

IDENTITY (*svabhāva*)   The "intrinsic identifiability" of anything. The ordinary mind compartmentalizes its experience into objects appearing to be independent entities. The inherent lack of identity in persons and things constitutes voidness, their true mode of existence.

ILLUSION, ILLUSORY (*bhranti, māyopama*)   Māyopama, "like a (magical) illusion" (*māyā-upama*), emphasizes the fact that the mind distorts experience of reality in the way a magician alters our perception of something. Our conditioned perception causes the world to appear as something which it is not.

ILLUSORY-BODY   The mentally controlled body of an accomplished yogin. (When unhyphenated, it indicates the ordinary body of an undeveloped being which takes its form through deluded preconceptions.) Synonym: rainbow-body, vajra-body.

IMPRINT (*Vāsanā*)   The mental traces of past experience and action which give rise to the present samsaric situation.

INSIGHT *see* Analytic Insight.

INSISTENCE (*abhiniveṣa*)   The automatic perceptual and conceptual belief in the existence of self and objects in the environment as independent identities; the way they appear due to the conditioned patterning of perception and thought.

JETSUN   Tibetan title of respect for advanced persons; in this book it refers to Milarepa.

KARMA   *see* Action.

KARMAMUDRĀ   Refers to the practice of sexual union in tantric yoga.

LAMA (*guru*)   Spiritual guide or teacher.

LOTSAWA (*lokachakṣur*)   Literally "eye for the world;" Tibetan title for translators of buddhist texts.

LOWER STATES (*durgati*)   *see* Six States.

MAHĀMUDRĀ   "Great Gesture" or "Great Seal." An advanced practice closely aligned with the Peerless (*anuttara*) Yoga Tantras; aimed at direct revelation of the natural reality of the apparent world.

MĀṆḌALA   The symbolic, graphic representation of a tantric deity's realm of existence. Also, the arrangement of offerings in tantric ritual (*pūja*).

MĀṆI-MANTRA   The mantra "Oṃ Māṇi Padme Hūṃ."

MANTRA   Sound in the form of syllables and words which can communicate the realities of tantric deities, grant supernormal powers (*siddhi*), or induce purification and realization.

MANTRA VEHICLE (*mantrayāna*)   *see* Vehicle.

MARPA   Milarepa's "root lama" or principal spiritual teacher.

METHOD (*upāya*)   The active expression of the mind-for-enlightenment (*bodhicitta*). It is the complement of transcendent wisdom which balances its intense revelations and which the bodhisattva uses to relate to beings, skillfully turning each situation into an opportunity for advancement for all.

MIND-FOR-ENLIGHTENMENT (*bodhicitta*)   The intent to attain one's own enlightenment in order to help liberate others. It is not the state of enlightenment itself, but the selfless drive to attain it for the sake of others. In the Great Vehicle it is the necessary complement to the penetrating insight into voidness, and in the Tantric Vehicle it is the prerequisite to real practice.

MUNDANE (*laukika*)   Perceptions, thoughts, emotions, and states of mind which occur under the influence of conditioning or imprinting of past experience; the apparent world.

NAGA (*nāga*)   Fabulous human-headed serpents of Indian mythology who dwell underwater in their own advanced civilization.

NĀROPA (*Nāropāda*)   Indian buddhist yogin (1016–1100) who was the teacher of Marpa, Milarepa's lama, and who brought together a number of yogic practices, now known as the "Six Yogas of Naropa," into an integrated adjunct to Mahāmudrā practice.

NATURAL STATE (*gnas.lugs*)   The natural mode of existence of all things; the mental state wherein experience is not distorted by preconceived perceptions of identities.

NIRVANA (*nirvāṇa*)   The cessation of one's own misery through eradication of afflictional mental states. In the Great Vehicle *nirvāṇa* is used in distinction to *enlightenment*, which involves not only the eradication of misery but also the attainment of unique abilities and insights into reality.

NONIDENTIFICATION (*niravalamba*)   In gnostic wisdom, the perception free from the preconceptual conditions which "create" the discrete, independent identities of the apparent world.

PATTERNING (*vikālpa*)   The structuring of cognition due to the traces of past experience; this patterning gives rise to the apparent world of self and environment and all our emotional reactions to such appearances.

PEERLESS TANTRA (*anuttara-yoga-tantra*)   The highest level of tantric teaching and practice, to which class the Mahāmudrā belongs.

PERSONAL DEITY (*iṣṭadevatā, yi.dam*)   Figures of the tantric pantheon who embody particular mental states and the practices leading to transformation of the practitioner's mind into the "mind of the deity." Usually a practitioner has a relationship with one particular deity, based on his personal nature and aims, although others may also be involved in practice over time. Through correct empowerment, instructions, and visualization meditation, a practitioner eventually experiences the deity and his mental reality.

POST-ATTAINMENT   The state immediately following any direct, transcendent experience of voidness, called "actual realization state." During the actual realization state the perception of the apparent world yields to the perception of its voidness, while in the post-attainment state the preconceived perception of the apparent world returns subtly altered by the preceding experience.

PRETA   "Frustrated spirit" *see* Six States.

PRODUCTION PHASE   *see* Two Phases.

REALITY-BODY   *see* Three Bodies.

REALITY-ELEMENT   *see* Dharma-realm.

REPA   A yogin who has activated the inner heat by tummo yoga and thus wears only a thin cotton robe, even in winter.

SAMSARA (*saṃsāra*)   Literally "to run around;" the condition of recurrent birth through the force of action (*karma*) and afflictive mental states. It applies to all states of existence of the three realms and their six life-forms.

SEED-SYLLABLE (*bīja*)   Monosyllabic mantric sounds embodying a universal principle, a deity's reality, or a psychic process.

SEVEN ENLIGHTENMENT FACTORS (*saptabodhyaṅga*)   Mindfulness, investigation, effort, joy, refinement and serenity, concentration, and equanimity.

SEVEN SUPERIOR TREASURES   Basic aids in all types of practice: faith, morality, modesty, receptiveness to Dharma, attentiveness, charity, and wisdom.

SHASTRA (*śastra*)   The works of Indian masters which develop, systematize, or clarify the original teachings of Shakyamuni Buddha.

SIDDHA   "Accomplished person," one who has achieved siddhis.

SIDDHI   The supernormal powers developed by the practice of yoga: clairvoyance, clairaudience, levitation, thought-reading, and control of the body and external world. All siddhis are mundane (samsaric) with the exception of the supreme siddhi, enlightenment.

SIX REALMS OF EXISTENCE   *see* Six States.

SIX STATES   The six states or classes of life forms of samsara: gods (*deva*), anti-gods, (*asura*), humans, animals, frustrated spirits (*preta*), and hell beings. The first three are called higher states and the last three lower states.

SIX TRANSCENDENCES (*pāramitā*)   Six integrated practices aimed at developing the stores of merit and gnosis: giving, morality, patience, vigor, concentration, and wisdom.

SMALL VEHICLE (*hīnayāna*)   *see* Vehicle.

SOLITARY-BUDDHA (*pratyeka-buddha*)   A person of the Small Vehicle who has attained nirvana for his own benefit without the aid of a buddha's teachings.

SPECIAL INTENT (*lhag.bsam*)   Intense concern for the miserable condition of others, leading to activation of great compassion.

STRUCTURING   *see* Patterning.

SUPERFICIAL REALITY, SUPERFICIAL WORLD (*saṁvṛtti-satya*)   The world as it appears when perception is conditioned by verbal conventions. The term *reality* emphasizes the fact that, owing to its relative self-consistency, it does appear to be a valid reality to ordinary beings.

SUPERIOR (*ārya*)   A person who has experienced voidness and has thus attained the "path of seeing."

SUPPLICATION (*praṇidhāna*)   Intercession with buddhas and bodhisattvas on behalf of all beings; aimed at providing for their welfare, both spiritual and temporal. "Supplication" denotes both the prayer and the mental resolution to aid beings, the latter replacing action (*karma*) and afflictive mental states in creating the rebirth and supernormal abilities of a bodhisattva.

SUTRA (*sūtra*)   The original, spoken scriptures of Shakyamuni Buddha. They are divided into three divisions or "Baskets": Instruction and Philosophy (*Sūtra*), Mental Science (*Abhidharma*), and Discipline (*Vinaya*).

SYNTHESIS (*saṁskara*)   "Compounded things," events or "objects" which arise through cause and effect and not through any intrinsic properties. All synthetic, or compounded, things must undergo dissolution at some time.

TANTRA   Scriptures of Shakyamuni and other buddhas relating to tantric, or esoteric, practice.

TANTRIC VEHICLE (*tantrayāna*)   *see* Vehicle.

TATHĀGĀTA   Epithet of a buddha; literally, "one who has gone there."

TEN EVILS (*akuśala*)   The ten main evils are killing, stealing, sexual misconduct, lying, slander, abusive speech, senseless speech, coveting, ill-will, and wrong views. The ten main virtues are abstaining from these evils.

TEN VIRTUES (*kuśala*)   *see* Ten Evils.

THREE BASES OF PRACTICE   Morality, concentration, and wisdom, which include all buddhist practices.

THREE BODIES (*trikāya*)   The three modes of existence and communication for an enlightened being. Dharma-body, or reality-body, is the embodiment of voidness and its realization; the enjoyment-body is the means of communication with advanced meditators; and the emanation-body appears like a physical body in the world, but its form and activities are consciously directed and consist of the training of undeveloped beings. A fourth body, the essential-body, represents the unity of the above three.

THREE COMMITMENTS (*saṁbara*)   The vow of personal liberation of the Small Vehicle, the bodhisattva vow of the Great Vehicle, and the tantric vows of the Tantric Vehicle.

THREE DISCIPLINES   *see* Three Bases of Practice.

THREE POISONS (OR FIVE) (*viṣa*)   The principal afflictive mental functions: ignorance, desire, and aversion, as well as jealousy and pride.

THREE REALMS (*tridhātu*)   The totality of samsara. The desire realm, so named because its inhabitants are primarily concerned with sensory gratification, includes beings of all six states of existence. The form and formless realms consist exclusively of gods whose mental states correspond to those of the eight absorption levels. The form realm corresponds to the first four absorption levels and the formless realm to the second four levels.

THREE WISDOMS   The wisdoms derived from learning, considering or reflecting on what was learned, and meditating with the principles thus considered comprise all knowledge and realization in the course of development. The first two are termed "mundane" because they are not transcendent, consisting of facts learned from reliable sources and those derived from rational consideration of them. When such correctly considered facts are applied in meditation, the resultant transcendent realization experiences are termed "wisdom derived from meditation."

TORMA   Small cakes of barley flour used as offerings during worship (*pūja*).

TRACE   *see* Imprint.

TRANQUILIZATION (*śamatha*)   The systematic quieting of mental activity through practice of one-pointed concentration. It is the means of attaining the eight absorption levels and the prerequisite for proper practice of analytic insight.

TRANSCENDENT (*lokottara*)   Mental events or experiences beyond the world of conditioned appearances (in other words, the experience of voidness).

TRIPLE GEM (*triratna*)   The refuge sources of buddhism: the Buddha, representing enlightenment; the Dharma, Buddha's teachings; and the Sangha, the community of practitioners.

TRUE BEING   Same as "reality-body" (*see* Three Bodies).

TUMMO HEAT (*caṇḍa*)   The inner heat developed by one type of tantric yoga.

TWO OBSCURATIONS (*avāraṇa*)   The afflictional obscuration (*kleśa-avāraṇa*) consists of negative mental states which obscure nirvana's freedom from misery. The objective obscuration (*jñeya-avāraṇa*) consists of fundamental misperceptions of the world which obscure perfect enlightenment.

TWO PHASES (*krama*)   The two stages of tantric practice. The first, the production phase (*utpatti-krama*), involves the visualized production of the tantric deities and their domains. The second, the completion phase (*utpanna-krama*), is the completion of this process by penetrating the voidness of all appearances.

TWO REALITIES (*satya-dvaya*)   The two modes of existence of phenomena. The superficial reality (*saṁvṛtti-satya*) is the world appearing in the form of independent identities to ordinary, undefective perception conditioned by preconceptions. Absolute reality (*paramārtha-satya*) is the voidness of all phenomena; that is, their inherent lack of independent identity.

TWO STORES (*saṁbhara*)   The two accumulations of personal power: the store of merit based on ethical behavior and ritual; and the store of gnosis based on knowledge and wisdom. When completed, the two stores provide the necessary elements utilized in achieving direct experience of voidness.

VAJRA   Symbol of the indestructible and indivisible reality represented variously as a scepter, a diamond, or a thunderbolt.

VAJRA-BODY (*vajrakāya*) *see* Illusory-body.

VAJRADHĀRA Transhistorical buddha who is the source of the Kagyupa lineage and teachings.

VAJRA HELL The lowest, most intense of the hells.

VEHICLE, THREE VEHICLES (*yāna*) The term *vehicle* connotes a means of traveling to enlightenment; that is, a major system of teaching and practice. The Small, or Elders' Vehicle is the oldest, relying on the scriptures set down in Pali. The Great Vehicle includes the teachings of the Small Vehicle, but in a new context and expanded scope. The Tantric Vehicle (synonym: Vajra Vehicle, Mantra Vehicle) combines the outlook of the Great Vehicle with a radically different, high-powered system of practice.

VOIDNESS (*śūnyatā*) The actual nature of all things; the lack of any independent ego of persons and identity of things.

WARRIOR (*dba'.bo*) Male tantric figure.

WHITE ELEMENT *see* Drops.

WISDOM (*prajñā*) Generally, any correct knowledge. Specifically, transcendent wisdom, the direct perception of the void nature of persons and things. During such experience the perception of the apparent world is temporarily suppressed.

YAKSHA (*yakṣa*) Destructive demons of Indian folklore.

Further Readings

Chang, Garma C. C., trans., *The Hundred Thousand Songs of Milarepa*, New Hyde Park, N.Y.: University Books, 1962

Dor-je, Wang-ch'ug, the Ninth Karmapa, *The Mahamudra Eliminating the Darkness of Ignorance*, translated by Alexander Berzin, Dharamsala: Library of Tibetan Works and Archives, 1978

Evans-Wentz, W. Y., ed., *Tibet's Great Yogi Milarepa*, London: Oxford, 1928

Freemantle, F. and C. Trungpa, trans., *The Tibetan Book of the Dead*, Boulder: Shambhala, 1975.

Gyatso, Geshe Kelsang, *Clear Light of Bliss*, London: Wisdom, 1982

Guenther, Herbert V., trans., *The Life and Teaching of Naropa*, London: Oxford, 1963

Heruka, Tsang Nyon, *The Life of Marpa the Translator*, Boulder: Prajna Press, 1982

Kongtrul, Jamgon, *The Torch of Certainty*, translated by Judith Hanson, Boulder: Shambhala, 1977

Kunga Rimpoche, Lama and Brian Cutillo, trans., *Drinking the Mountain Stream*, New York: Lotsawa, 1978

Lhalungpa, Lobsang P., trans., *The Life of Milarepa*, New York: E. P. Dutton, 1977

Sangpo Rinbochay, Khetsum, *Tantric Practice in Nyingma*, translated by Jeffrey Hopkins, London: Rider, 1982

sGam.po.pa, *The Jewel Ornament of Liberation*, translated by Herbert V. Guenther, Berkeley: Shambhala, 1971

Taranatha, Jo Nang, *The Seven Instruction Lineages*, translated by David Templeman, Dharamsala: Library of Tibetan Works and Archives, 1983

Trungpa, Chogyam, ed., *The Rain of Wisdom*, Boulder: Shambhala, 1980